He grabbed her shoulders, and for a moment his thoughts stopped. Her skin was as soft as it looked and she smelled good. Something faintly sweet but not perfumed. She smelled like something he would love to bury his face in and inhale. "You can't drown yourself yet. There's a basket filled with Swiss chocolates waiting inside for you."

She placed her hands over her face, her voice coming out muffled. "Oh, please tell me you don't have a basket of chocolates waiting inside. I said so many things to you. So many stupid, stupid things."

"You called me a sexy shortstop with a squeezable behind."

She groaned. "Don't remind me."

He pulled her hands away from her face. "Look at me, Ms. Andersen."

She shook her head, her eyes still shut. "Call me Virginia. After all I've said to you, I think you've more than earned the right to call me by my first name."

"Open your eyes." He was touching her. He had just met her and yet he had her hands in his. He knew he should drop them, but he wanted to see her eyes again.

Dear Reader,

Welcome to Hideaway Island. Home of crystal-blue waters, white sandy beaches and the Bradley siblings. Join them on their journeys of self-discovery as they fall in love in one of the most beautiful places in the world.

In *Surrender at Sunset* meet Carlos, the superstar baseball player who's hiding from the world after a career-ending injury. His new spunky decorator, Virginia, knows her biggest job will be to show Carlos that the simplest things in life are often the most meaningful.

Jamie Pope

SURRENDER
AT SUNSET

Jamie Pope

 HARLEQUIN® KIMANI™ ROMANCE

Recycling programs
for this product may
not exist in your area.

ISBN-13: 978-0-373-86438-6

Surrender at Sunset

HARLEQUIN®

www.Harlequin.com

Printed in U.S.A.

Jamie Pope first fell in love with romance when her mother placed a novel in her hands at the age of thirteen. She became addicted to love stories and has been writing them ever since. When she's not writing her next book, you can find her shopping for shoes or binge-watching shows on Netflix.

Books by Jamie Pope

Harlequin Kimani Romance

Surrender at Sunset

To the Harlequin Kimani team.
Thanks for all your support.

Acknowledgments

Jamie B., Denise S., Gail C., Jen M., Heidi U.
Thanks for brainstorming with me in Vermont.

Chapter 1

Carlos Bradley heard the faint sounds of voices coming from somewhere in his house as he lay in his bed. One male and one female. For a moment he was mildly curious as to whom the voices belonged to. He lived on the secluded side of a small island off the Florida coast. He had picked the location because it was almost jungle-like. Hot and overgrown and tropical. At times he felt as if he was the only one on Earth. No guests. No visitors allowed. Just a cleaning woman and a groundskeeper who came once every other week.

It must be them talking. None of his friends would come down here, even though they had offered once they had learned of his bad news. But after a while the offers had stopped. His phone no longer rang. He was alone. As he wanted to be.

He pulled the covers over his head in a vain attempt to block out the bright sun that was streaming through his bedroom windows and tried to go back to sleep. It was probably well past noon, but he wanted darkness. Night was the only time he could shut his eyes and forget that the world was still going on without him.

"Carlos!" He heard the voice of his baby sister, Ava, and then felt her bounce onto the bed. "This bed is enormous. Is he even in here?"

"Yeah," his brother and Ava's twin, Elias, answered. "He's the lump in the middle." A hard fist came down on his shoulder.

The hit stung but Carlos, too tired to even make noise, said nothing, just pulled the covers away from his face and glared at his younger siblings. "What..." His mouth felt dry. His tongue heavy from not having been used in so long. He couldn't remember the last time he had spoken to anybody, much less carried on a conversation.

"What the hell are you doing here?" The twins were the only ones who still came around. They both led busy lives so he didn't see them much. But they were the only ones who attempted to keep his connection to the outside world.

"We came to see what you were up to." Ava gave him a once-over, concern in her eyes that hadn't shown up in her voice. "You look terrible."

"You look like shit," Elias said, staring at him.

"I'm healing. Get the hell out." He turned over and put a pillow over his face. He didn't want to see anybody. He didn't want to be around anybody. That was why he had escaped instead of staying in Miami, where all of his friends, colleagues and fans were. Why hadn't they gotten that through their thick heads by now?

"And I thought you were Mr. MVP. Mr. All-American.

Mr. Super Nice Guy Baseball Hero." Elias shook his head. "If your fans could see you now."

His fans.

They wouldn't want to see him now. They wouldn't want to see him at all. Not like this. Not broken and useless.

He had only been good for one thing, and that was winning games. Now that he couldn't do that anymore, what was his purpose?

He *was* Mr. MVP, a star player since the day he'd picked up a glove. But that had all ended when his Achilles tendon had ruptured during the playoff game that had taken his team, the Miami Hammerheads, to the World Series. Surgery, rehab and six months away from baseball, and all he had to show for it was a nasty scar and decreased range of motion.

"How's your foot?" Elias asked him, seeming to have read his mind. His brother grabbed his leg and studied the scar on his heel. Carlos could have fought the examination, but frankly he was too tired to give a damn. Plus, Elias was a doctor, in his first year of surgical residency. Even though his brother was a pain in his ass right now, he trusted his opinion.

Elias pushed back on his toes, causing a slight twinge in his tendon that hadn't gone away since the operation. "Feels really tight," Elias said, rotating his foot. "Are you doing your exercises?"

He was quiet. He had been good about it until a few weeks ago, until his father's birthday arrived and it had hit him. He no longer had the two things that mattered most in his life. His father and the game.

Nothing seemed important anymore.

"That's such a nasty scar," Ava said, touching it. "He

went to the best of the best, you'd think they'd find a way to make the scar look better."

"It would have been better if Mr. Overachiever here hadn't overdone it after the surgery. Thought he could go back normal activity, just like that. The wound got infected. You did more damage than good by overworking it."

"Thanks for the recap. Now get out." He didn't need the reminder. He knew he had screwed things up, but he'd wanted to go back so badly. It was bad enough that he'd missed the game of his life. He hadn't wanted to miss the next season. But instead of a quick recovery it had been setback after setback.

"You know how many hours I work. I barely get a day off. When I do, I come all the way from Miami to see you, the least you could do is be hospitable. Offer us some coffee. How about some lunch? A glass of lemonade? Something." Elias looked down at him, annoyed.

"What do you want?"

"To see you, big brother." Ava snuggled closer to him, resting her head on his shoulder. "Mom was asking about you."

"I just talked to Mom. She's having a nice time in Costa Rica with her sisters."

"Yes, but since we live in the same state she thinks that we should spend time with you. I know you'd much rather be left alone, but I'm more scared of her than you. So we're here. Get over it."

Carlos sighed and wrapped his arm around Ava. He'd always had a soft spot for his baby sister. She had still been in college when their had father passed away, and at nine years her senior he had stepped in over the years in their father's absence. "She is scary," he admitted with a sigh.

"She's started working out," Elias said. "If I didn't have a foot and a hundred pounds on her, I'm pretty sure she could take me."

"Get up, Carlos," Ava said, rising from the bed. "Feed us. I do love this island but it's a pain to get here."

It looked as though Carlos didn't have much of a choice. Sometimes he viewed his younger siblings like a bad rash. Hard to get rid of. Everybody else had easily faded away once he'd gotten injured, but Elias and Ava had never left. And they wouldn't leave him today until he got out of bed.

He forced himself past the immediate, familiar feeling of tightness in his heel as he set his feet on the floor. One of the reasons he'd bought this house was because of the huge master suite. It contained a bedroom, bathroom and sitting room, and with the small fridge he kept in there, he didn't have to leave it for days at a time.

The house was enormous, much bigger than one man would ever need. But he had bought it because his father had liked it. It was oceanfront, secluded. The landscape around it made him feel as if he were in an undeveloped tropical country instead of on a little island off the coast of South Florida. His father had said it was a place that he could see a family spending their summers. He'd said it was a place built for a superstar. Carlos had bought it, thinking that his parents would spend their winters there and that the family would gather there for holidays. But when his father had died from a massive heart attack that had all changed.

His mother spent most of her time traveling around the world. Too active to stay still. Too sad to be around anything that reminded her of her husband. His older sister stayed in their native Maryland with her growing family who had their own traditions now. Elias was always working or studying, and Ava… Ava dated rich men. The house had stayed mostly empty for the past five years, but when Carlos had got hurt and Miami had become too much, it had been the only place he could think to go.

"I don't think I have much to offer you," he said as he led them into the massive kitchen. "I've got frozen pizza." He opened the freezer, revealing that it was stacked to the top with them.

"Why do you have so much pizza?" Ava asked. Carlos looked back at his sister, who was dressed head to toe in designer wear. She was a beautiful girl and she knew it. She spent most of her days maintaining her beauty. He would guess that nothing processed and frozen had passed her lips in years.

"I was the spokesman for their brand. They do a lot for pediatric cancer research so I donated my fee and they gave me a lifetime's supply of pizza."

"Oh, do you have any fresh spinach? I could go for a simple spinach salad."

"No." He preheated the oven and went back to the refrigerator. "It's either a sports drink or water. Take your pick."

Elias grinned at him. "I'll take a red one if you've got it. Ignore Miss Priss over here. Pizza is fine. Her rich fiancé can take her out to dinner later and feed her all the salad she wants."

"Speaking of rich fiancés." Ava looped her arm through his. "We've been searching for venues to get married next year and we are having a really hard time finding one we like."

"You mean one *you* like." Elias shook his head. "Your man doesn't give a damn where you get married. I think he would be happy going to city hall and saving a hundred grand."

"Nobody is talking to you, Eli."

"Oh, excuse me? Did I need to wait to be called on? I hadn't realized that we were back in elementary school."

"Cool it, you two," Carlos said firmly. He knew his siblings could go at it for hours once they got started, but they were closer to each other than to anybody else on the planet. They went to the same college and even now they lived next door to each other in matching town houses.

"He started it." Ava looked at Eli.

"Well, I'm finishing it. What were you saying, Ava?"

"I've loved this island since Daddy first brought us here as kids. I want to get married here, but there is no venue that's large enough." She looked up at him with the big, soulful brown eyes that had gotten her out of a lot of trouble when she was a kid. "But this place looks as if it could easily hold two hundred and fifty guests."

"You want to get married here?" He wasn't sure why he was surprised to hear that. She was the one who'd suggested he look for a house on this island five years ago.

"Yes, and I came to ask you to walk me down the aisle. Will you?"

He was surprisingly touched by her question. It seemed as if the only things he'd felt the past few months were anger and emptiness. "What about Mom? I thought she was going to walk you."

"I want you to do it. You take care of me. And if Daddy can't be there I want his favorite person in the world to."

"Okay," he said. It was all he could say. He couldn't turn her down, even if he wanted to.

Her eyes lit. "Okay to walking me down the aisle? Or okay to me having the wedding here?"

"Okay to both." His father would have wanted it that way. He would have wanted his baby girl to marry in a place that she loved, and it was Carlos's job to make sure all of his father's dreams came true. Even if he wasn't around to see them anymore.

"Thank you, Carlos!" She pulled him into a hard hug. "You going to fix up this place before the wedding, right?"

"Fix it up?" He looked around him. There was barely any furniture and the walls were white and bare but it looked fine to him.

"Yes, fix it up. Make it look more like a home than an abandoned oceanfront warehouse."

"I've got to agree with Ava on that one. This house looks like a big, expensive dump."

"Dump? It might be a bit sparse, but it's not a dump."

The twins looked at each other, communicating without words in a way that always drove him crazy.

"Fine. Whatever. I'll fix it up. What do you think I should do with it?"

"I don't know." Elias shrugged. "It's your place."

"Get an interior designer." Ava rolled her eyes.

"A what?"

"A decorator. You know, a professional person who will make this place look less like a rich serial killer lives here and more like the superstar athlete you are."

"Where do I get one of those? The phone book?"

"The internet?" Elias suggested.

Ava rolled her eyes. "You don't just pick a stranger. You get a personal recommendation."

"From who, exactly?"

"I don't know." She went into the freezer, took a pie out and placed in the oven. "Don't you have friends that have homes you like? You could ask one of them."

"I never paid attention to their houses." He truthfully had not. Plus, a lot of his player friends were married. Their wives took control of most of the household stuff.

"Well, what about your condo in Miami? Who did that?" Elias asked.

"It came like that. I bought the model unit."

They all were quiet for a moment. "What about that little inn we rented out for Mommy's birthday? It had just been redone. You liked it there, Carlos. I can call and find out who did it."

He had liked it there. It was so different from all the other places in Miami, unlike all the other places he had stayed while on vacation. He had felt truly relaxed then, one of the rare times he'd felt that way since he became a man. He couldn't describe what the place had looked like, but it had had a homeyness to it that had made him not want to leave.

"Okay. Let me know who it is and I'll set it up."

Virginia Andersen rubbed her forehead as she re-entered her tiny rented office. The Miami heat and the stress of the day were finally getting to her. She had just returned from Mrs. Westerfield's house for the second time that day after spending two hours showing her drape samples.

In every color imaginable.

It wasn't as if Virginia minded showing the elderly woman the drapes. It was her job as an interior designer to do so. And since Mrs. Westerfield was her only paying client at the moment, she didn't really have a choice. She just had one complaint. It was a small one, really. The elderly woman used her more like a personal assistant than an interior designer. Virginia walked her bichon frise, went to the grocery store with her and helped her picked out what to wear on her dates with someone she referred to as her gentlemen caller. And none of that bothered her. Mrs. Westerfield was fabulous with her love of vintage clothes, art and Latin culture. It was just…

It wasn't her job.

And when her parents called to see what she was working on—and they always wanted to know what she was working on—she wanted to tell them she was using her eye for design and color to decorate beautiful homes, not picking up dog mess.

It was important to her that she prove to her parents that she was successful, or at least supporting herself in a lifestyle that they saw fit. Her father was a high-ranking military official, and her mother was a mathematics professor at an Ivy League college back in her home state of New Jersey. They'd had big plans for their twins.

But none of them included being an almost starving artist, and that was just what Virginia had been before she'd opened her design firm. Moving from state to state, chasing boyfriend after artistic boyfriend and painting. Some of her pieces had sold for big bucks, but it was never enough for her parents. They'd never understand her need to splash colors onto a blank canvas. They were too practical to see how a painting on a wall could bring someone joy.

And while they would have much rather had her be an actuary or an engineer, they'd never denied her the opportunity to learn about the things she loved. She had a bachelor of fine arts in painting with a minor in interior design and a master's degree in art history. She was educated, just like any child of Colonel and

Dr. Andersen should be, and they felt she should have a job suited to that education.

She'd been all ready to ignore her parents' wishes and follow her heart, until her heart had led her here to Miami. She had come here at the request of her last boyfriend. Burcet, a beautiful Moroccan man with striking bronzed skin and long, wavy black hair, had grown up in France and spoke the most perfect French. He was a sculptor, passionate about his work and incredibly sweet and sensitive.

She had followed him when he'd told her he was going to get his big break, asking her to support his dreams, promising that once he hit it big he would return the favor. But after six months here he had disappeared, leaving a goodbye note taped to her microwave, never telling her why he left, just saying that he couldn't be his true self with her.

That was when she'd taken a long hard look at her life. She'd been twenty-eight then, sleeping on a mattress in an un-air-conditioned studio apartment because she'd wanted to live the bohemian-artist lifestyle. And because she'd thought she was in love. But what had she had to show for it?

Absolutely nothing but the thoughts her parents had put in her mind about coming back home and getting a sensible job and leading a sensible life.

But *sensible* meant *boring* to her. So she'd taken her savings and her design degree and decided to do something meaningful. She'd opened a design firm. But for the past year she'd only had a few high-paying jobs in Miami's crowded market. Most of her clients of late were the little elderly ladies who lived in Mrs. Westerfield's condo complex. And while she enjoyed doing neoclassic dining rooms, she wanted a project that she could really sink her teeth into. She'd only had a couple of those and she was afraid there weren't going to be many more in her future. If things didn't pick up, she was going to have move back home and get that practical job her parents were always suggesting. Her mother had an in at a university. Virginia could be teaching bored college freshman Art History 101 by fall. All she had to do was say the word. All she had to do was go home with her tail tucked between her legs.

But she didn't want that. She wanted a career where she could be creative. Where she could be in charge of her own path.

The phone on her desk rang and she jumped. Mrs. Westerfield had her cell phone number, so it couldn't be her. Her heart lifted at the thought of a new client. "Andersen Interiors. How can I help you today?"

"I've got a German shepherd that needs to be taken to the vet. Are you available?"

"Shut up, Asa," she said to her twin brother, but she smiled as she said it. Her brother was the only one who really understood her because he'd been raised by the same parents with the same expectations.

He chuckled. "What's going on with you today, Gin? I called your cell but it went to voice mail."

"That's because I took Mrs. Westerfield to get a pedicure and had to shut off my phone."

"You took her to get a pedicure?"

"Yup. She wanted me there to help her pick out a color. One that went with her manicure but not one that matched exactly. Coordination is in, matching is out, apparently. Then, this afternoon she called me back and fed me excellent chicken salad and lemonade while we looked at drapes. She's tired of the ones in her bedroom. In fact, she's tired of her bedroom, period, and would either like a Paris in the twenties theme or a hard-bodied man to shake things up." She doodled a sketch on a piece of paper as she spoke to him. "You keep yourself in good shape, why don't you truck yourself down here and make yourself useful?"

"No, thanks. Why do you work for her anyway?"

"Because, believe it or not, I like her and she pays me for my time. I told her she didn't have to anymore, but she says she's rich and she can't take it with her, and she likes having a decorator on retainer. Plus she feeds me. She's taking gourmet cooking classes and she tries all her new recipes out on me."

"Sounds as if she's keeping active in her old age."

"I want to be her when I grow up," Virginia told him, meaning it. "She's going on a world cruise next week. She'll be gone for one hundred and eight days. I'm going to miss her."

"What are you going to do without your only paying customer?"

"Panhandle? Do caricatures on the boardwalk? I hear they are looking for cage dancers at a bar downtown."

"Or you could come home," he said quietly. "Well, not home to Mom and Dad, but move to New York where I am. You could be with all your artsy people and I'm sure you could get a job teaching at a school here without Mom's help."

"I don't want to teach, Asa. I like being an interior designer. I'm good at it, too. I just need more time to prove it."

"I know, Gin. You're a good painter, too. A great one, but you gave that up." He knew she had to follow her own path, just as he had to follow his. He'd been on track to become a doctor, just the way her parents wanted, but he'd dropped out of medical school in his third year and become a paramedic. He was too much of an adrenaline junkie to do rounds and spend all day in one building. His choice had, of course, disappointed their parents. Both of them had disappointed their parents when they'd diverged from the paths laid out before them. "You do whatever you want, Gin. But you can always come home if you need to."

"I know."

"I know you know. Just don't forget it. I've got to go. I'm about to start my shift."

"Love you."

"Yeah, me, too." They disconnected. Asa used to drive her crazy when they were kids, but they had grown a lot closer as adults, though they lived hundreds of miles away from each other. He was protective, even though she was older by six minutes. He would make a good husband for some woman.

One day.

It was as if her brother was on a single-handed mission to date all the women in the mid-Atlantic states.

Her phone rang again, which was shocking considering she barely got two calls a week, much less two in one day. "Andersen Interiors. How can I help you today?"

"Is Virginia Andersen there?" It was a man's deep voice, one that sounded vaguely familiar but she couldn't place.

"This is she."

"This is the same Virginia Andersen who did the Rosecove Inn?"

"Yes, I was the interior designer." Rosecove had been her favorite job. There was something special about that little ocean-side inn with its own private beach. It had been one of her first big jobs, and the owner had taken a chance on her. She'd be forever grateful for that chance. When she'd showed her parents the pictures of it afterward they had been impressed. She didn't need their praise to feel validated, but it sure was nice to have it.

"Good. I want you to decorate my house."

"You do?" She tried to keep the surprise out of her voice. "Great! Are you interested in your entire home or just a few rooms?"

"The entire thing."

Her heart beat a little faster as she changed the page on her notepad. This was just what she needed. A new client equaled a new opportunity. "How many bedrooms?"

"Six bedrooms. Five bathrooms."

"Six bedrooms, five bathrooms?" Her voice squeaked. "How many square feet are we talking, Mr...."

"Mr. Bradley and seventeen thousand."

"Square feet?" she squeaked. "Seventeen as in one more than sixteen and one less than eighteen."

"Yes," he said slowly, and she realized something was up. This was a joke... It had to be. She didn't know whether to laugh at the absurdity of it all or cry, because for a moment she'd thought she had the job of her dreams.

"Your house is seventeen thousand square feet and you want me, who has decorated two inns and a slew of old ladies' condos, to decorate it? Okay, Mr. Bradley, my mysterious benefactor, who are you really?"

"I'm Carlos Bradley." His deep voice sounded slightly annoyed. "I have a house on Hideaway Island that I would like you to decorate."

"Carlos Bradley! The sexy shortstop." She laughed. "You look damn good in those uniform pants, Mr. Bradley. Tell me, how many squats does it take to get your behind that hard?"

"Excuse me?"

"You've got a great butt. One that I would very much like to squeeze one day."

"Uh…I might let you one day, but I think we should at least meet first to talk about the house."

"Your house. Right. I suppose I have an unlimited budget to decorate your massive mansion. Tell me, do you have a pool and a tennis court that need some jazzing up, too?"

"Yes to the unlimited budget and pool, and no to the tennis court."

"Can I ask you a personal question, Carlos?"

"You told me you wanted to squeeze my ass, I think we're at that stage in our relationship."

"Do you really give gift baskets to all the women you sleep with after you're done with them?"

"Where did you hear that?"

"Where any self-respecting gossip seeker does. The internet. There was a picture of one and everything."

"I don't give every woman a gift basket."

"It depends on how good they are in bed, huh?"

"What?"

She giggled. She would think this was a mean joke if she weren't so entertained by it. "You can drop the act now. Are you one of Asa's friends? You've done a great job mimicking the voice. I'm impressed."

"I'm sorry, Ms. Andersen, but this is *really* Carlos Bradley and I *really* am calling to see if you will decorate my house."

"Yeah, yeah." She rolled her eyes. "And I was on the cover of the swimsuit issue."

"I'm not joking."

"No? Well, if you aren't joking and you are Mr. MVP with the sexy round behind and the sleazy parting gifts, then I expect a town car waiting for me here at ten to-morrow morning and a private plane taking me to Hide-away Island. I could take the ferry, but why should I? You can afford to fly me out."

"A private plane?"

"Yup and chocolate. I would like a basket of Swiss chocolates waiting for me when I get there."

"Fine. 10:00 a.m. I'll see you tomorrow."

"Great! See ya then." She hung up the phone. Asa had gotten her good. She was going to have fun get-ting him back.

Chapter 2

The next morning Virginia was sitting in her office thumbing through her recently delivered design magazines when a man in a black suit and cap came through the door.

"Can I help you?"

"I'm here to pick up Virginia Andersen."

She blinked at the man for a moment. He certainly was wearing a driver's uniform complete with a name tag. "Pick me up for what?"

"I'm Mr. Bradley's Miami driver. He asked me to take you to the airstrip. There will be another driver waiting for you to take you to his house."

"What?" She laughed. "You're here to take me to the airstrip?"

"Yes, ma'am." He looked confused for a moment and then glanced at his watch. "The pickup was requested for ten o'clock. Is that correct?"

"Um…" She thought back to the phone call yesterday. She had requested a 10:00 a.m. pickup along with a long list of ridiculous things. Her brother had sworn he wasn't playing a joke on her when she'd called him last night. She hadn't believed him. He was the same guy who used to throw spiders at her when they were kids. She wouldn't put a phone call past him, but this… this was too much. "I did say ten."

"Do you need more time, ma'am?"

"No." She stood up, grabbing her handbag from beneath her desk. "I just need to lock up. I'll be out in a minute."

"I'll be waiting outside." He turned to leave.

"Wait! You aren't an ax murderer, are you?"

"No," he said slowly, pulling out his wallet. "I can show you my credentials." He showed her his employee ID and his driver's license.

"You probably think I sound crazy. You probably are just doing what you are paid to do and have nothing to do with this whatsoever. I'll be out in a moment. Thank you, Richard."

He left and Virginia pulled her cell phone out of her bag, calling her best friend Willa.

"Hello?"

"Hey, Wil. It's me. I can't talk right now, but I think my brother is playing a huge joke on me. Just in case he's not, I want someone to know that a driver showed up at my office to take me to Carlos Bradley's house. The story is he wants me to decorate it."

"What?"

"I know." Virginia shook her head. "It's unbelievable. But if I don't call you back by eight tonight, call the police."

"Don't get in that car, girl. It could be because I write

murder mysteries for a living that I'm crazy paranoid, but I wouldn't do it."

"I really think Asa's up to something. He called me yesterday right before all this started. He wanted me to come home. I'm wondering what it is."

"He wants you home? Okay. Go, but you better call me long before eight."

Willa was smart, the calm, sensible counterpart to Virginia's adventurous nature. "Okay. I'll call you after each leg of the trip."

"Each leg? Where the hell are you going?"

"I think I might be headed to Hideaway Island."

Carlos sat just outside his front door waiting to see if the interior designer actually showed up. He could have waited in his house for her, but curiosity about the woman he'd had the strangest conversation of his life with had driven him outdoors.

He couldn't remember the last time he'd just sat outside and let the sun beat down on his back. It had probably been the last time he was on the field, the same day he'd got hurt. He had spent so much of his life outside, smelling Astroturf, sweat and dirt, hearing thousands of fans cheer whenever he stepped up to bat. But it had all ended abruptly. Surgery, rehab, recovery. No fields, no fans, no career. It didn't seem as if it made much sense for him to go outside anymore. But this morning the air-conditioning inside had become too much for him. The stuffy, too-chilled air had made him feel a little choked, so he'd escaped outside, sitting on the stone steps that led to his front door.

He had to admit that the heat felt good, the sun felt good, and the air, even though it wasn't dirt, sweat and grass scented the way he was used to, smelled sweet

to him. Like ocean air. Like summer. He might still
be sitting in his bedroom trying to block the sun out if
it weren't for his siblings and the crazy designer who
didn't believe he'd called her.

He could have hung up, called around, hired somebody else who had a better résumé. It would have been
a hell of a lot less trouble. But there was something
about Virginia's voice on the phone, something about
her warm laughter that made him want to meet her. If
for nothing more than to put a face to the woman who'd
told him she wanted to squeeze his butt.

People didn't talk to him like that. At least, not to
his face, and he found that intriguing.

A black town car pulled up. Its windows were down,
revealing the passenger in the backseat. Carlos couldn't
see her features clearly but he could see that her skin
was just a shade lighter than milk chocolate and her
hair was in wild thick curls.

The car then came to a stop, the woman scrambling
out before the driver could reach her. She was pretty.
Beautiful, really, but in an earthy unglamorous way
that he wasn't used to. She wore a long, light pink dress
with big flowers, and it bared her pretty shoulders and
hugged her curvy body in all the right places. Her skin
looked smooth and sun kissed. He wasn't sure what he'd
been expecting. Maybe someone older. Maybe someone more polished. Not a woman staring up at his house
with eyes wide and her mouth open.

He stood up, walking down the steps to meet her.
She hadn't seemed to notice him until that moment.
Her eyes snapped to his face. Beautiful almond-shaped
eyes with thick lashes. As he stepped closer he could
see that her face was clean of makeup, her cheekbones
were sharp, but her face wasn't thin. *Nice* didn't seem

like a good enough word, but she was nice to look at. Like somebody he could spend hours observing and never get tired of the image.

"Holy crap. It *is* you." She surprised him by touching his arm; not just touching it, but wrapping her fingers around his biceps. "Wow, that's hard." She took her hand away and he found immediately that he missed the contact. It had been so long since he had been touched. "You're real, right? I'm not dreaming or hallucinating. You're really Carlos Bradley, and you really wanted me to decorate your house."

"You thought I was lying?"

She slowly closed her eyes as a flush spread over her face. "I thought my twin brother was playing a huge joke on me."

"You have a twin?"

"Yes, Asa. I called him last night promising retribution. He probably thinks I'm a nutcase. You probably think I'm a nutcase."

"I do. But I have twin siblings, so I understand."

She opened her eyes, looking thoroughly embarrassed and really kind of adorable. "Thank you for being understanding. If you could be so kind as to point me toward the ocean."

"It's behind the house."

"Great." She stepped away from him. "If you need me, I'll just be drowning myself in it."

He grabbed her shoulders and for a moment his thoughts stopped. Her skin was as soft as it looked, and she smelled good. Something faintly sweet but not perfumed. She smelled like something he would love to bury his face in and inhale. "You can't drown yourself yet. There's a basket filled with Swiss chocolates waiting inside for you."

She placed her hands over her face, her voice coming out muffled. "Oh, please tell me you don't have a basket of chocolates waiting inside. I said so many things to you. So many stupid, stupid things."

"You called me a sexy shortstop with a squeezable ass."

She groaned. "Don't remind me."

He pulled her hands away from her face. "Look at me, Ms. Andersen."

She shook her head, her eyes still shut. "Call me Virginia. After all I've said to you I think you've more than earned the right to call me by my first name."

"Open your eyes." He was touching her, he had just met her and yet he had her hands in his. He knew he should drop them, but he wanted to see her eyes again.

"I don't want to."

This had to be a dream. It had to be. Stuff like this just didn't happen to her. She didn't arrive in chauffeured cars or ride in private jets. Especially not for work. She was usually chauffeuring people around. She had even picked up Mrs. Westerfield at the airport on a few occasions. But now she was standing in front of the biggest house she had ever seen, with America's favorite baseball player holding on to her hands. She didn't want to open her eyes. Because when she did, she would have to come face-to-face with the fact that she had just blown the opportunity at the job of a lifetime.

"It's hot out here," Carlos said. "Come inside."

She opened her eyes then, and there he was. Mr. MVP. He was royalty in Miami, a legend in the making, so she'd seen his image everywhere. Billboards. Commercials. In magazines. Still, she hadn't paid much attention. She knew less about baseball than she knew about quantum physics. The only things she knew about him were that he was rich, he was good at his job and he went through more women than he did pairs of underwear.

That put him in her "typical womanizing athlete" category. Somebody she wouldn't find attractive no matter how good-looking they were. But the thing was, he was extraordinarily handsome in person. Nowhere in sight was that plastered-on smiling face that she saw in ads. The real deal wasn't smiling at all. He was looking at her with intense green eyes that contrasted with his deep brown skin. He was big, too. Well over six feet tall with a hard body that heat just seemed to roll off. He was one beautiful man, and he was touching her, holding her smaller hands in his massive ones. She'd be a big fat liar if she said her tummy didn't feel a little funny.

"Okay." She tried to compose herself as she followed him in, but she couldn't stop the barrage of berating thoughts that kept entering her head. She was dressed well enough to take Mrs. Westerfield around town, but not to meet an important client. She would have worn a suit. She would have tamed her wild hair.

Her mother's voice kept playing in her head.

If you want to be a professional you have to look professional.

Virginia had never seen a hair out of place on her mother's head. She would pass out if she knew that Virginia was here in a maxi dress with bare shoulders and strappy sandals. It didn't matter anyway. She wasn't going to get this job.

She shouldn't get this job. She really wasn't qualified. Carlos's home was a Spanish-style mansion with a beautiful roof of handmade red tiles. It was art. Everything from the rounded windows to the heavy wood carved door and meticulously placed stone accents was perfectly planned. It was such a contrast with its surroundings, which were kind of wild and unkempt. Coming to Hideaway Island felt like coming to another world, but coming to Carlos's quiet part of the island was something else entirely. It almost felt like a fantasy.

She followed him to the foyer, which was big, open and airy with high ceilings but nothing else. No colors on the walls, no art, nothing. It was truly a blank slate. A dozen ideas rushed into her head. There were so many things she could do with this space alone.

She walked a little farther into the house, into a great room that held a single couch. Nothing else. Their footsteps echoed around her in the empty room. The architecture of the inside of the house was as beautiful as the outside, but that was it. The place was empty, but more than that, it felt empty. "Are you living here at the moment?"

"Yes," he answered, looking back at her.

"Alone?"

"Yeah."

"Oh, but this place is so big for you to be here alone," she said as she walked into the kitchen. "It's so secluded here. Don't you get lonely?"

He stopped fully, turning to face her. She'd known it was a stupid question as soon as it came out of her mouth. She had no right to ask him. "It's none of my business," she said in a rush. "You could probably have a different woman here every night of the week if you wanted." He just blinked at her and she wished she had a muzzle, something to shove in her mouth to keep her from speaking. She just couldn't get over the fact that she was here with him. Here alone with him, on this secluded island, in the middle of nowhere.

"I came here because I wanted to get away from everything."

"I understand," she said quietly. It might have been all in her mind, but he had this way of looking at her. Maybe it was his intense green eyes, but he looked at her in a way no other man had. In a way that made her skin hot. In a way that made her want to get closer to him and run away at the same time.

She was attracted to him and it was weird. She liked artsy men. Dancers, painters and poets with soulful eyes and sensitive hearts, and yet this massive athlete with his quiet manner and stern face was making her tingle with just a look.

"I bought this house five years ago, but because of my schedule I haven't stayed here. I'm only here now because I'm no longer playing."

"You're not playing?"

He looked at her blankly. "It's baseball season and I'm here."

"It's baseball season?"

"Are you serious?"

"Um, yes," she answered feeling dumber by the moment.

"Do you even know what team I play for, Ms. Andersen?"

"The Dolphins?"

"That's football." He shook his head. "I play for the Hammerheads. I ruptured my Achilles tendon going for a catch in the playoff game that took my team to the World Series. I had surgery and an infection. They haven't cleared me to play this year. It was reported everywhere."

"I guess I've been paying more attention to your behind than your career, because I didn't know any of that." She shook her head immediately. "I don't know why I can't control my mouth around you. Yes, I do. I've been spending too much time with Mrs. Westerfield."

"Who's Mrs. Westerfield?" he asked, looking bewildered.

"My client. She's seventy-eight and has no filters. Said she's lived through two husbands and five wars and has earned the right to say whatever she pleases. My parents would be horrified if they could see me right now. Totally horrified. Why aren't you telling me to shut up?" She was babbling, but there was something about him that made her nervous.

He shook his head and gently grabbed her wrist. "Let's go see the rest of the house."

"I came all the way out here. I might as well." He looked at her strangely, but she ignored it. He was touching her again with his big, callous, rough hand that felt good on her sensitive skin. It made her wonder how his hands would feel grazing over her hips or on the backs of her thighs. She tried to shake off that thought. But it was too good. One day she was going to tell her grandchildren about the day a baseball legend had grabbed her hand and showed her around his house.

"There are two bedrooms down that hallway." He motioned with his head as he walked. "One's a suite with a bathroom. There's another full bathroom down that hall for guests to use."

He led her into a large open room where one wall was a row of doors that opened onto a lavish pool that overlooked the ocean. There was no other way to describe it but luxurious. With a few changes and some bikini-clad women it could be the setting for a glossy music video. She understood why he'd bought this place. It was fit for a superstar like him.

"This is beautiful," she told him.

He nodded and led her out of the door, past the pool and onto the path that led to the beach. Away from the lavishness of the house, the land around them was wild, not landscaped, but it was probably one of the most beautiful spots in the country. The other side of the island, where she'd landed, was adorable, with a cute little shops and restaurants and a downtown that had a European feel. It wasn't as touristy as some of the other islands off the coast. It was quiet. But on this side of the island she felt truly at peace, with the sound of the waves crashing against the shore and the breeze blowing through her hair. She felt relaxed for the first time since the car showed up at her door that morning. Which was odd, because she was standing next to a gorgeous millionaire, someone she had made a fool out of herself in front of.

"My little sister wants to get married here next year. She wants me to walk her down the aisle. I need the house fixed up before then, so she can impress all of his important friends. It's very important to me that she is happy."

"Who's she marrying?"

"Some older man. He's a real estate investor from England who wants to take over all of South Florida."

"You don't sound as though you're too fond of him."

"He spoils the hell out of her and she seems happy. She's got him opening up a restaurant here on the island next season. But no, I don't like him. I don't trust him. He's forty-nine. She's twenty-seven. What the hell does he want with her?"

"Aren't you a hypocrite? Wasn't the last woman you dated twenty-one?"

He looked at her again, those piercing eyes of his

narrowing. "You know that, but you don't know that I got hurt or what team I played for?"

She shrugged. "I remember being irrationally annoyed at you when I heard that on some entertainment news show. You're a thirty-six-year-old grown man and she's barely out of girlhood. Someone who should be studying for her college final instead of spread across the hood of a car in a bathing suit that would fit a toddler. What the hell did you want with her? I've seen that girl give an interview. Don't tell me it was for her sparkling conversation."

"She was more mature than most her age and I was with her because I know she didn't want me for my money."

"No. She wanted you for your status. Every up-and-coming model needs to be seen on the arm of a major athlete.

"Has anyone ever accused you of overstepping? Because you seem to have a knack for it."

She knew she was wrong. She knew she had crossed a line, but she couldn't stop herself with him. She couldn't make herself shut up. He probably didn't run into too many women like her. He was a mythic figure to most of the world, and she should probably be cowed by him, but for some reason she wasn't.

"I'm probably never going to see you again. What's the harm?"

"What do you mean you're not going to see me again? How are you going to decorate my house?"

"What?" She shook her head, thinking she must be hearing things.

"I want you to decorate my house. I told you I needed it done before my sister's wedding next year."

"But—but…are you sure? I've never done anything

of this size. And you haven't seen my portfolio. And there is the fact that I've acted like a complete crazy person the whole time we've been acquainted."

"But you did Rosecove?"

"Yes."

"Then, you have the job. I wouldn't have gone through all the trouble of bringing you in unless I was going to hire you."

"Oh." She didn't know what to say. This was the job of her dreams. This was the job that would keep her business open and her parents off her back. This was the job that could take her career to the next level, and she was stupidly talking herself out of it.

"You do want the job, don't you?"

"Um, yeah."

"Yeah? You don't sound too sure. If you don't think you can handle it, I can find someone else."

"Of course I want this job, Mr. Bradley. I won't disappoint you."

"Good. It's yours."

Her heart jumped into her throat. She couldn't believe it. She was on a beautiful island and had just been offered the job that could make her career. It seemed too good to be true. "Could you excuse me for a moment? I just have to make a phone call."

She walked away from him, back up the path toward the house as she pulled out her cell phone.

Willa picked up on the first ring. "You're alive?"

"Yes, and I'm walking away from the beach toward the biggest house on the planet. He offered me the job, Wils!"

"Why?" She didn't sound at all impressed.

"What do you mean, why?"

"You've done a couple of beachside inns and you specialize in old-lady condos. Why does he want you? Are you sure he's not some kind of serial killer who lures interior designers to his secluded estate and then collects their body parts in jars in his basement? That's a great idea for a book. I'll call it *Designed for Murder*."

"Could you stop being a mystery writer for one moment and be my supportive best friend?" Virginia asked, even though she knew Willa was right. There were a hundred other designers more qualified than she.

"Yeah. I guess I could do that. This is an amazing opportunity that could skyrocket your career. And I think that deserves a happy dance." Virginia heard Willa switch her phone to speaker. "Come on, girl. I'd better not be dancing alone here. Shake what your mama gave you."

Virginia laughed, just imagining Willa in front of her desk in her little New York apartment dancing to celebrate her success. They had happy danced when Willa had gotten her first book deal. "I got the job," she sang as she shook her hips. "I got the job." Now they were dancing for her.

Carlos came up behind Virginia only to catch her dancing as she held the phone to her ear. A foreign sound escaped his mouth and he realized that he was laughing. She had done that to him, made him see the humor in something when for so long he hadn't been able to find anything to bring a smile to his face. But she'd done it. She was the only one who'd managed it, even though others had tried. She was just herself. Her blunt, quirky self. Maybe he was crazy to offer her the job on the spot. She could be a maniac. But he wanted her, and he always got what he wanted.

Her back was to him so she couldn't see him, and

he was glad because he got to look at her shaking her rump as long as he wanted. He knew her dance wasn't meant to be seductive, but he felt himself harden. It may have been because she was woman and he was a man who had gone a long time without one. But it had to be more than that. She'd called him out on dating a twenty-one-year-old model and she was right. Looking at her now, that girl couldn't compare to her. No swimsuit model could.

He wondered what was going on under that long dress. Were her legs as shapely as her hips? Was the skin on her chest as smooth as the skin on her shoulders looked? Did her behind look as luscious and round as it appeared through all that fabric?

She turned around suddenly, her mouth open slightly. She had pretty lips. He had noticed that about her, too.

"Gotta go, Wils. He caught me."

He could hear the sound of feminine laughter before they disconnected.

"I promise I'll be professional while I'm on this job. I have references if you want to check. I'm always on time. I mind my manners and I'm efficient."

"I don't care if you like to dance on the job as long as you get it done. That means not having me wait fourteen months for some lamps. No renovations that are going to take longer than a year."

"I understand. I know some great contractors."

"Good, and you stay out of my bedroom. I don't want it touched and I don't want to be bothered during the day. If you've got a problem, handle it yourself."

"Okay." She nodded.

"One more thing. You've got to live here." He'd thought about putting her up in town, but that was a twenty-minute drive every day. It just made sense to keep her closer.

"Live here? I've never lived with a client before."

"There's a first time for everything. Do you agree to that stipulation?"

She hesitated for a moment. "Yes. I agree."

"Good. You'll take the suite on the first floor. I'll call the car back for you. You start on Monday."

Chapter 3

Virginia arrived at Carlos's door that Monday with her entire life in two large suitcases. She was going to be living there for the next few months, with a man she only knew bits and pieces about from the things she heard on TV or read on the internet. Part of her was nervous about it. This job was so huge. It could change the course of her career or be a huge, epic failure.

Virginia was used to epic failures. All her past relationships were. Her former life as a painter was, too, according to her mother. She'd tried to put that behind her, but as she was driven down the long single-lane road that led to Carlos's house she couldn't help but be moved by the natural raw beauty of the island. It made her wonder what this island would look like depicted in oils.

She didn't normally do landscapes. She preferred people and capturing emotion on canvas, but her fingers itched to pick up a paintbrush and capture the emotion of the land, the rich green from the palm trees, the bursts of bright pink from the flowers. The ocean at sunrise. Or the waves that crashed against the shore at sunset. There was so much to see, she thought she might never tire of looking at it all. But she wasn't there to paint. She had a job to do.

The front door opened and Carlos stood there. He wore another T-shirt and shorts. His feet were in sneakers. Everything about him screamed *jock*. And everything, from the way he held his powerful body to the way he looked at her, was appealing. Which was ironic, because he was exactly the type of guy she would have stayed away from in high school and college. Now he was making her hormones go crazy. Maybe it had been too long since her last relationship. Maybe she was in serious need of some sexual release.

It couldn't happen with him, though. He was a client. She might drive some of her past clients to the airport and clean up after their dogs, but sleeping with them was where she drew the line. Of course, none of her other clients looked like exotic hard-bodied gods. But that didn't matter, because even if she'd been less than professional getting the job, she would be on her best behavior during it.

"Were you going to ring the bell or just stand there all day?"

"Sorry. I was thinking. How did you know I was here?"

"Cameras." He took the largest suitcase away from her as he studied her.

She was normally a fairly confident person, but the way he looked at her made her feel a little like a self-conscious thirteen-year-old again. But she was dressed smartly today. No flowy hippie dress. No wild untamed curls. She wore gray slacks and a turquoise blouse with a delicate bow at the collar. Her skin was completely covered and she would have worn a blazer if the Florida humidity hadn't been a touch too much.

"Why are you so dressed up today?" He stepped aside, letting her into the house.

"Despite the way I acted the first time we met, I assure you I am a professional. And from here on out I plan to treat you with the respect you deserve, the respect I would give to any other client."

He kicked the door closed, not looking at all impressed by her statement. "If you would have shown up her the other day wearing this shirt, I wouldn't have hired you." He walked away from her, deeper into the house.

"What? Why?" She followed, looking down at her shirt. It wasn't her personal style but there was nothing offensive about it.

"It's stupid."

"My mother bought me this shirt and she's the smartest person I know. I'm going to tell her you said that."

He looked back at her. The corner of his mouth had curved into a smile and she just about fainted right there on the spot. He was a beautiful man, there was no denying that, but when he smiled at her the way he did, with just a tiny bit of mischief in his eyes, he was damn sexy.

"I'm not afraid of your mother. I think I can handle her."

"Do you? I'm afraid of her. Think you can give me a few tips?"

His smile widened and, if possible, grew sexier. It caused heat to spread through her belly, and she knew she was in trouble. Never in her life had a simple smile aroused her. But Carlos Bradley seemed to make impossible things happen to her. "My mother can be scary, too. I've got nothing for you."

Leaving her suitcase near the door, he took her through the great room again, and this time she noted the two beautiful winding staircases that led to the second floor and a massive fireplace with an intricately carved mantel in the center of the back wall. She'd been so overwhelmed the first time she was there she hadn't been able to take it all in, but now she could see the details, the little things that made the place special.

He took her down the long hallway that they had passed on the way to the family room the other day. There were marble floors in different shades of creams and tans, and a little sitting area by the elegantly curved window in the middle of it all that showed distant views of the ocean. "It's so private back here," she said, more to herself than to him. "You would barely know if someone else was home."

"My father thought it was perfect. There are four of us. He said there was enough space so that none of us would fight, and if we did he would send us to our rooms."

There was a sadness in his voice as he said it, and she knew he had suffered a loss. "Did you fight a lot when you were kids?"

"Normal amount, I guess. We lived in a tiny three-bedroom house. There was just no getting away from each other." He opened the door to the room at the very end of the hall and she was blown away at the bedroom before her. "This is your room."

Room was an understatement, with the sitting area and the patio that led out to the pool. It was twice the size of her apartment. "This is amazing."

"I hope you are comfortable here."

"There's not a strong enough word to tell you how I feel about this room."

He nodded as if he were pleased by her answer and stepped forward, his hand raised. She wasn't sure what he was going to do, but she held her breath as he grew closer, her heart beating a little quicker. He yanked the little bow at her throat, causing it to come loose and reveal the top of her chest. If it were anybody else she might have smacked them, but her chest felt looser, as if that little bow had been choking her.

"That's better. I can't look at you with that stupid bow." His fingers lingered where they were, his knuckles pressed against her skin. Her nipples grew tight. She didn't want him to remove his hand, but instead slide it down so that she could feel it in more than just one spot.

But that was a bad thought. She worked for him. He was her boss and she needed to keep her attraction to him in check no matter how tempting it was to jump off the deep end and onto him. Taking both of her hands, she wrapped them around his larger one and slowly pulled it away from her chest. "I didn't know you were such a fashion critic."

"It makes me doubt your taste, and since you are decorating my house that's a concern for me."

"Well, the wonderful thing about this being your house is that I will decorate it however you want. What is your vision for this place?"

"I have no vision. That why I hired you."

"You have no idea at all? What about furniture? What about paint colors?"

"This is the room my mother or sister will stay in, so I want it to be made up for a woman. Other than that I don't care what you do. Just make it nice. I don't want any updates. I don't want to know what you're doing, just show me when you're done."

"You want a big reveal?" she asked, flabbergasted. "But you live here. It's going to be hard to surprise you."

"I don't want anything done to the kitchen I mostly keep to my bedroom and the gym. There's also a theater room on the other side of the house that I might be in. But other than that I'll stay out of your way. And, during the day, you stay out of mine."

"Okay." She nodded, even though it was going to be hard to make this place over without any direction from him at all.

"I have a credit card for you to use. There's some cash for your expenses. There's no budget, but I have cut you a check for half of your fee. If you don't think it's fair we can negotiate a higher price. Other than that, treat the house as if it were your own. The pool, kitchen and grounds are available to you. There's a car in the garage for your use."

"Okay." She nodded again, not knowing what else to say.

"I'll get you bags and leave you alone to get settled." He walked out, and she was glad he did because she had just become overwhelmed by it all. This house, this job, was too big for her. It was so unlike the little beachside inns she loved doing, a far cry from the three-room condos she was used to. A house like this should have a team of designers, or at least somebody with more experience. But she didn't have more experience and there was nobody else but her here to do it. So she was going to have to suck up her fears and get it done. Because she'd never quit a job in her life and she would be damned if this was her first.

* * *

Carlos left Virginia alone in her room. He knew he had gone a step too far when he'd unraveled that silly little bow on her shirt. But he hadn't been able to help himself. It was as if his fingers had developed a mind of their own, eager to reveal the woman he had met a few days ago. The woman he couldn't stop thinking about, even though he desperately tried to. She had come covered up today—long sleeves, long pants, closed-toe heels. Her hair was pinned back. Her wild curls hidden from him. He didn't like it. The raw, earthy beauty she had was gone, and left was another professional-looking woman who was a dime a dozen.

He could tell she was subdued today, trying to be the person she thought should be instead of the woman she really was. He didn't want normal. He didn't want professional. If he had, he would have hung up on her the day he called. He never would have gone through the trouble of bringing her here in the first place.

And so when he'd been in her bedroom with her, he hadn't been able to resist messing her up a little, revealing her a little. It was a mistake, because the backs of his fingers had touched the soft skin of her chest. It had taken everything inside him not to slide his hand just a little lower and pop open some of her buttons. He knew if he had, he wouldn't have been satisfied with just looking at her. He would have wanted to run his fingers over the top of her cleavage, maybe lower his lips to her chest and kiss her there.

Kissing that lush body wouldn't have been enough. There was the bed there, just across the room. It had stood before him like a big neon sign, beckoning him. All he'd have had to do was lift her off her feet and carry her there. All he'd have had to do was strip away those layers of clothes and cover her body with his own, satisfying a need he hadn't known he'd had until she'd walked into his world.

But he had hired her to work for him and he knew that he shouldn't cross that line, especially before one wall was painted. For now he just needed to keep out of her way and keep his hands off her.

Virginia changed out of the outfit that Carlos seemed to hate so much and spent the rest of the day wandering the house with her sketch pad in hand, making notes and just imagining what the space could be.

He was a superstar, an athlete and a legend in the making. Plus, he was a single man in the prime of his life. His house should reflect that. The common spaces were going to have to be sleek and sophisticated enough to impress any one of the important guests at his sister's wedding, but she would make the bedrooms homey. Each one of them different and reflective of the beautiful setting around them.

Around six that night she left the dining room and went into the kitchen that, despite being renovated five years ago, looked as modern as some of the work she had recently done. Finished in a rich mahogany, it was a cook's dream with its huge granite-top island, double ovens, multiple sinks and spacious countertops. It seemed like a waste for a single man.

Her stomach rumbled. Carlos had never mentioned anything about food, not that she was expecting him to provide her with meals, but she wondered what she was going to eat tonight. She opened the refrigerator door to find it filled with sport drinks and water. There were a couple of bottles of expensive imported beer, but not much else. Not even eggs. The freezer was full of

frozen pizza. There were hot dogs there, too, and that
left her wondering what the man ate. She opened the
cabinets to see only protein bars and a large jar of pea-
nut butter. Shaking her head, she changed the page on
her pad and started making a list.

"Why are you shaking your head?"

She looked up to see Carlos standing in the doorway of the far side of the kitchen; the house was so big
she hadn't heard his footsteps. "I was just wondering
how you keep your body so hard when you eat like a
thirteen-year-old boy."

"I thought I was eating pretty well," he said as he
stepped closer. "There's no marshmallow cereal or in-
stant cups of soup in there." He stopped next to her, his
body so close that his arm brushed against hers as he
looked down at her list. She had changed into shorts
and a tank top, a far cry from what she'd been wearing
when she'd arrived. The brush of his skin against hers
caused goose bumps to break out on her skin.

"Thank heaven for small miracles. I'm going to make
a grocery store run."

"You don't have to. I can have whatever you want
delivered."

"And let somebody else choose my fruit? You must
be crazy. There's a grocery store in town, right?"

"There's two. One that sells gourmet stuff. The other
is where most of the locals go. Just tell the car's GPS
where you want it to go and it will lead you there."

"Or you could lead me there." She didn't know why
she'd issued the invitation, but the thought of leaving
him alone in this huge house didn't sit well with her.

"No."

She was taken aback by his brisk refusal. "No? It
will be dark by the time I get back. I was hoping there

would be less of a chance getting lost on the island if you come with me."

"You can wait until morning to go. There's enough food here for the night."

"I just thought you could show me around a little."

"It's not my job to show you around," he said coldly. "I'm paying you for a service and that's it. You have three choices. Take your chances alone in town tonight. Go in the morning. Or make a list of things you need and I'll have them delivered. I'm not going into town."

"Okay. I'm sorry. I'll go in the morning."

He nodded. "If you're hungry, the frozen pizza isn't bad." He walked away then, leaving Virginia a little bit heartsore and a hell of a lot confused.

Chapter 4

Carlos woke up the next morning feeling like a world-class asshole. He had been rude to Virginia last night. Incredibly rude, and if his father had heard him he would have smacked him in the mouth.

She'd just wanted to go to the supermarket. It wasn't a strange request; it wasn't something that would require a lot out of him. Buying groceries was something that normal people did, but he hadn't been normal in a very long time. And he hadn't been off his property since he'd heard that the team's doctors weren't removing him from the injured list.

There was no need to leave here. There was nothing he had to do. No schedule he had to keep. Even before he left Miami he'd never ventured into a store. Everything he needed was delivered to him. All he had to do was pick up the phone.

It wasn't as if he could just leave the house and go to

the supermarket like anybody else. He'd stopped being able to the day he'd been drafted to the majors right out of high school. He wasn't able to go to the park with his siblings without somebody recognizing him. He hadn't been able to go to dinner in a normal chain restaurant without being mobbed by fans.

He had loved it, at first. He was grateful for all the love and support from his fans, but when he'd got hurt all that had changed. Now all people wanted to know was when he was coming back. When he was going to take his team to the playoffs again.

He didn't have an answer for them. His parents had both worked two jobs to move them to a better neighborhood. His sister taught at-risk kids. His little brother was studying to be a surgeon. All he had to do was play baseball. And now that he couldn't, he felt a little like a failure. He had lost the ability to do the thing that had made his father swell with pride every time he saw him play. Maybe he was on Hideaway Island to escape all of that, the expectation, the disappointment, now that he couldn't give people what they wanted. He couldn't do the only thing he had ever been good at.

That was why he had balked when Virginia had asked him to go grocery shopping with her. He couldn't remember the last time he'd left the house, much less gone out in public.

He went downstairs looking for her. She wasn't in the kitchen, the dining room or the living room. Her bedroom was empty, her bed made up, the room clean as if no one had slept in it.

The house felt empty. Unlike last night. The house had felt different; it hadn't felt as empty. He hadn't felt as empty, knowing she was there. But now he wondered if she had gone, quit because he was the asshole who didn't want to leave his house. He walked outside by the pool area, finding it empty, but then he spotted a little pair of gold sandals in the sand on the path that led to the beach.

As he walked down the pathway, seeing her foot-prints, his chest began to feel looser. And there she was, sitting at the edge of the water, her feet being splashed by the waves. Her dress was bunched up at her waist and she seemed lost in thought.

He kicked off his sneakers and sat beside her. The sand was damp, the water cool, but it was a shock to his system. He hadn't done this before. He had what most people dream of—a private beach. Half an island to himself. Unspoiled nature surrounding him, and yet he had never sat outside and enjoyed it. Never felt the sand between his toes, never smelled the sweet, salty air, never looked out on the endless blue ocean that was right outside his home.

He felt guilty because he was here to enjoy this place when his father couldn't. His father would be so disappointed to see that he hadn't even bothered to go outside and just breathe it all in.

"I've never been on a beach alone," she said to him after a moment. "Especially a beach like this. It's truly something, isn't it?"

"It's beautiful. How long have you been out here?"

"Since the sun came up. I couldn't sleep last night so I came out here to think."

"To think," he repeated. "About what?"

"About this job. About whether I've gotten in over my head. I was thinking about if maybe I should leave."

He was quiet for a moment, knowing he needed to apologize for snapping at her last night, but not knowing how to begin. "Do you want to leave?"

"I feel as if I'm intruding, Mr. Bradley."

"I feel as if you're supposed to call me Carlos." He stood up, extending his hand. "Come to the market with me."

He had a Range Rover in the garage solely for her use, but she wanted to him to drive the old-school black convertible that was big as a tank and took as much gas. It had come with the house; the former owner had fixed it up himself.

"I'm feeling a little like Lena Horne in the 1950s," she said as the ocean air whipped around them. "Just give me a big pair of sunglasses and a fabulous scarf." She had her bare feet up on the dashboard, those long shapely legs stretched out before him, distracting his attention from the road. He was very tempted to run his hand up one of them, just to feel more of her softness, but he stopped himself. Never in his life had he met anyone he wanted to touch more; never in his life had he found a woman so tempting.

"I never would have thought to come here until you called me," she said, looking at the scenery around her. "This doesn't feel like Florida. It feels as if I'm in another country altogether."

"My parents brought us here once, as kids. So when the opportunity came up to buy it, I did."

"I would have loved to come here as a kid," she said wistfully. "My parents aren't the relax-on-the-beach, sand-between-their-toes type of people."

"My mother is from Costa Rica. She had a hard time living in Maryland, away from the water, so every summer my parents would pack us in the car and drive us down to Florida. My father loved the beach. He saved all his vacation days for the year so we could spend

two weeks down here. He would park his chair in the
sand in the morning and wouldn't leave until sundown
that night," he said, finding himself sharing more about
himself than he meant to.

"What did the rest of you do?" she asked, smiling.

"Ran wild." Memories came flooding back to him
of Ava and Elias running around the beach with inflat-
able water tubes around their waists, and his older sister
reading in the shade of an umbrella.

"I'm jealous." She shut her eyes and leaned back in
the seat, letting the rays of the sun hit her face. "My
parents were all about culture and educational vaca-
tions. As an adult I can appreciate seeing Prague. As a
seven-year-old, I'd much rather have gone to an amuse-
ment park on the Jersey Shore."

"Your parents took you to Europe as a kid?"

"Yes, my mother is a mathematics professor who
teaches courses with names like Complex Functions
Theories and Partial Differential Equations. My father
was a high-ranking military man and dealt with a lot of
foreign officials. They wanted their children to be well-
rounded individuals who could excel in any setting."

"Are you?"

"You've met me. What do you think? My parents
were expecting a doctor and another professor in the
family. But my brother is a paramedic and I decorate
people's houses for a living."

"You think they are disappointed in you?"

"Oh, I know they are, but I learned a long time ago
that I have to follow my dreams, not the dreams they
have for me."

He pulled into town and was greeted with the sight of
brightly colored buildings in mint greens, bright blues
and yellows. There were people strolling up and down

the small streets and diners eating on restaurant patios, but it wasn't crowded. It didn't feel like the height of tourist season, which it was. The whole place felt relaxed, a throwback to another time, and Carlos felt himself growing relaxed. He didn't think he would like being in town. But this place was so different from Miami. He forgot that was why he was drawn to it in the first place.

A few minutes later they were in the market, with him pushing the cart while Virginia went through her list.

"You aren't one of those low fat/no fat people, are you?" She stopped in front of the milk case.

"I've been known to enjoy a glass of two percent, but I can deal with the whole stuff."

"Good. I'm for veggies and healthy stuff, but when I cook, I like my cheese, my milk and my butter full of fat." She grinned. "I should have had that same mantra when it comes to men. I think I would have been a lot happier."

"You like your men skinny?"

"I used to like them skinny, artsy and a little bit smelly. I went through a phase. It started when I turned eighteen and ended when my last boyfriend dumped me a year ago."

"You're playing with me, right?"

"Unfortunately, no. He broke up with me by leaving a note on my microwave, and to top it all off, he stole my cat."

"He stole your cat?"

"Yeah. She hissed at me every time I came near her and had a weak bladder, but she was my cat and I tolerated her."

"Son of a bitch." He hadn't known her long, only for

a few days, but he knew that the guy who'd broken up with her was nothing but a loser and she was better off without him. "I hope you didn't cry over him."

She was smiling at him, and he lifted his hand to stroke his thumb across her cheek.

He was touching her again. In a way that a man shouldn't be touching the woman he'd just hired. Especially when that man had warned himself to stay away from her.

"I didn't. I'm just glad he didn't take the microwave," she said, sounding kind of breathless. "I would have missed my microwave."

They stood there for a moment, somehow getting closer. Her eyes went to his lips, and he wondered if she wanted the same thing he did. He wondered if she wanted him to close the distance between them and kiss the lips that looked so inviting.

Her stomach growled, breaking the moment and causing her to laugh. "Come on and let's hurry up in here so we can feed me."

It was for the best. He shouldn't be kissing her in public, in front of the dairy case in the store. He shouldn't be kissing her at all.

Virginia's cell phone rang from the pocket of her dress. It had been ringing all morning. She had put out so many calls, most of them local, trying to find residents of Hideaway Island who were skilled enough to do the work this house required. She'd found a few leads but she was hoping for more.

Pulling her phone out, she glanced at the screen and saw that it was her mother. She had barely spoken to her mother in the past few weeks, avoiding her calls. She had never been completely on board with Virginia becoming and interior designer. She had been thrilled to learn that Virginia had given up painting, but disappointed that she was choosing another career where her paychecks didn't come steadily every two weeks.

"Hello, Mother dearest."

"Please, Virginia, you know I dislike it when you call me that."

"I do. How are you?"

"I'm fine, dear. I'm calling you from the car. I'm headed to hear Stanislav Smirnov speak on percolation theory. I'm so excited. I've been anxiously awaiting my chance to hear him speak. I haven't heard a lecture of this level since I went to that symposium on combinatorics and number theory."

"That's great, Mom," Virginia said, having no clue what her mother was talking about. "I hope you have a good time. Tell me all about it later." She was prepared to disconnect, but she would have been getting off too easy.

"I didn't just call to tell you about that. I wanted to see how you were doing."

"I'm fine."

"But you're living with that baseball man now," Dr. Anderson said, the disapproval heavy in her voice.

"I'm redesigning his house."

"Yes, and the last man you lived with, you were giving art lessons to."

"That was different. He came to me to learn about color theory and we were in a relationship."

"He was an out-of-work sculptor with poor hygiene."

"You're right, Mother," Virginia said, in hopes they could just drop this line of conversation.

"You didn't mention to me you were going to be

living with this man. You have a way of glossing over those bits of information that I find truly astounding."

"I'm not living with him. I live downstairs in the back of his very large house. He lives upstairs. I'm just the help. I rarely see him and I promise you I am not sleeping with him."

"Who is this man anyway, Virginia? You're my only daughter and the light of my life. I don't like the idea of you living on a strange island with a man you don't know."

"I have to live here. His house is very far from town and he's not exactly a stranger."

"So you do know him. Aha! How long have you've been seeing him?"

"Mother! I'm not dating him and have no plans to. He's famous. Look him up. Carlos Bradley. Daddy knows who he is."

"Hmm." Her mother fell silent for a moment. "I know you've just started this job, sweetheart, but if you ever feel the need to come home, your father and I are here. You can even live with us as long as you need to. I can get you set up with a job. Perhaps introduce you to a nice stable man. There's a physicist here who is handsome and charming."

"A charming physicist? Isn't that an oxymoron?"

"Oh, Virginia. It's not. He would be a much better choice in a partner than some professional athlete. Even the kind ones are womanizers. All that time on the road. All those groupies."

"I'm not dating him, Mom. I don't plan on dating him or sleeping with him. I'm going to do this job and do it well because it can mean a lot for my design firm. I'll have enough money from this to live comfortably for a long time and you won't have to worry about me."

"I always worry about you. I always will. I'm your mother, and it's my most important job and the greatest thing I will ever do. You understand that, don't you?"

"I do."

"I love you."

"I love you, too, Mom. I've got to get back to work."

"All right, darling. Just remember you're welcome home anytime."

"I know. I'll talk to you later. Goodbye." Virginia hung up and walked out of the spare bedroom she was making sketches of. She wasn't sure how to feel about the conversation she had just had. Her parents were there for her. She could come home if she wanted. She guessed that, in the back of her mind, she'd always known that. There were some days, when she'd had no work at all, that she'd seriously thought about going back to New Jersey, to her father, who was always calm, reliable and strong, to her mother, who was always so sure about everything. But she knew she would suffocate there.

She needed to be creative. She needed to work in a job where she didn't do the same thing every day. That was why this job was so important to her. She had to do a good job. She had to do things the right way. She didn't want her mother to think that she had failed at this, too.

She walked back into the great room to see movers hard at work. The first item on her to-do list was to have the house painted. Painting a house this size was going to take some time, but she had to get rid all the furniture that she wasn't going to use. As first glance there hadn't seemed like much, but there was. It was just engulfed in a house of this size.

"Are you sure you two can carry that table? It's, like, a thousand pounds."

"You don't have to worry about us, ma'am. If we can't handle this you get your money back." One of the moving guys winked at her. He was cute, with brown skin, a baby face and dimples. His partner was blond haired, blue eyed and equally adorable. She was trying to hire as many local people as possible while she worked on this house instead of hiring people from off island. And the recent college grads' moving company seemed grateful for the work.

She had learned browsing the internet that Hideaway Island had some great craftsmen. The mayor of this island made furniture from salvaged wood that was some of the most beautiful work she had ever seen. She wished she could fill the entire house with it, but she knew that to create a look fit for the house of a superstar she was going to have to go in a different, grander direction.

But for the sleeping areas and smaller spaces she was going to use as many handcrafted items as she could. This might be a mansion fit for a king, but some parts of it should still feel homey.

She watched the movers carefully flip over the table and screw the legs off. "And you're sure this stuff will find a good home? I'd hate to see any of it thrown away."

"Yes, ma'am," the blond one said with a little bit of a Southern drawl. "The mayor collects furniture, and what he doesn't use in his business he donates to families in need. There was a bad fire on the island a few months ago that burned down three homes. The mayor is helping those people rebuild. I'm sure they would appreciate this furniture."

"Do they need anything else?" She heard Carlos's soft, deep voice behind her and she felt a tiny bit of...

she wasn't sure what to label it. Excitement? Delight? Like being in high school and seeing your crush at his locker? Even to her ears that seemed corny. It was just that she rarely saw him during the days. Sometimes he would pass her on his way to his gym, but most of the time she didn't see or hear from him until sunset, when he would emerge from whatever it was he was doing and seek food.

She liked that time of day. Most of her mornings were spent on the phone with suppliers and contractors, but she felt isolated in this big house. As beautiful and peaceful as it was, it wasn't Miami. She was okay with her own company, but she didn't like feeling alone in this house. She wondered how he could live for so long without human interaction.

"I don't know for sure, sir," the mover said slowly. By the look in his eyes she could tell he was starstruck. "I—I could ask the mayor."

"Please do. I would like to help, if I can."

The kid nodded. "I know this may not seem the most professional thing to do, but can I shake your hand?"

Carlos nodded and extended his head. "It's nice to meet you..."

"Brady," he said. "That's my partner, Sam. We're honored to work for you, sir. Real honored. I just about cried when I saw you go down in that playoff game. My mama even said a prayer for you when she heard you were going into surgery."

"I appreciate that," Carlos said quietly, but he had a slight pained look in his eyes. There was a shyness to him, a humbleness that she didn't expect from a pro athlete, and she found it very appealing.

"We promise to do a good job."

"I know you'll work hard for me. Thanks, fellas."

Brady smiled and nodded. "Come on, Sam. Let's get this stuff on the truck."

They hoisted up the tabletop and went out the door, each of them grinning and whispering.

"I guess they didn't expect to see you."

"I wasn't expecting to make an appearance." He looked at her again. His eyes swept over her body, taking her in as he did every time he saw her. In the way that caused goose bumps to break out on her flesh. She had never dressed for a man, and she wasn't going to start now, but part of her wondered if he approved of what he saw. She dressed comfortably, like herself. Not the way she had on her first day here. If there was one thing she'd learned about the man in her short time here, it was that he only wanted her to be herself.

"You were nice to him."

"Of course I was nice to him. My mother raised me right. You're getting rid of the furniture?"

"Yes. Was there anything you wanted to keep?"

"No." He shook his head. "No."

A long moment of silence stretched between them. Why was he here now? He had spent the day away from her, avoiding her, it seemed. She had tried a couple of times to update him on her work, but he'd never seemed interested, never seemed to care what she was doing. Some designers might love having such freedom, but it made her crazy never knowing if she was doing something he would like. It made him one of the hardest clients she'd ever had. She wasn't really working for him or with him. She was just on her own. "Was there something you wanted from me?"

"Maybe I just wanted to see you."

"Considering that you avoid me like the plague most of the time, I doubt it."

He stepped closer to her and she could feel the warm of his body in the cool air-conditioned room. If she stepped just a few inches toward him, closed the gap between them, her chest would be pressed against his. She wondered what that would feel like, his muscled body against hers, wondered what his skin would feel like, his strong back under her hands. Would it be just as hard as the rest of him looked? A vision of herself in bed, legs wrapped around him, digging her nails into his hard, muscled back popped into her head.

It made her tremble a bit. The vision was vivid, powerful and unexpected. She looked up into his eyes, her mouth going dry. He was looking at her in that way again, the way that made her uncomfortable, the way that made her feel as if he could see inside her. As though he knew what she was thinking.

She couldn't let him know what she was thinking.

She couldn't let him know how much he affected her. No man had ever moved her physically like this before. "What is it that you really want?" She tried to laugh, injecting humor into her voice as she took a slight step back and crossed her arms over her chest. Her nipples had grown tight. She hoped that they weren't visible through the thin material of her dress. She hoped he hadn't realized that he turned her on by doing nothing but standing there. "Did you come to ask me if there were any more brownies? Because I ate them all."

She had made brownies for them after they'd got home from the market the other day. The day she'd doubted her decision to work there. He had gone so cold on her when she'd asked him to go to the store with her. But then she'd had to remember that he wasn't like her other clients. He wasn't like the sweet elderly women who wanted her more for her time than her skills. She had overstepped by asking him to do anything with her.

But he had gone with her the next day, and she'd noticed his unease grow as they'd got closer to town, noticed how he only guided the cart down empty aisles. Just as his discomfort seemed to have grown when the mover had talked about his injury. That made her realize that it must be hard for him to be reminded of one of the most painful moments in his life every time he stepped out of the house. Maybe that was why he never left his home. It appeared that everything he wanted came to him.

He grabbed one of her curls and wrapped it around his finger as he inched his face closer to hers. The action made all the thoughts drain out of her head. "It would have been polite to ask me if I wanted the last one before you ate it."

"Oh?" She lifted her head, her heart beating a little faster. "You're going to school me on what polite is? Considering you ate ten of them, I thought it was okay if I polished off the last one. I actually, dare I say it, thought you might have saved the last one for me. It's what a gentleman would do."

He tugged on her hair, bringing her face a little closer to his. Her eyes went to his lips, to his smooth, full, brown lips that looked entirely kissable. Her mouth was inches from his and she could feel the heat of his face on hers. All she had to do was close the gap. All she had to do was take one more step forward.

"Um, excuse me?"

She jumped away from him, like a kid who'd got caught with her hand in the candy jar. This was exactly the thing her mother was worried about her doing. And Carlos was exactly the type of man she was worried about Virginia doing *it* with. She turned around expecting to see the movers, but instead there was a young man in a blue-checked button-down shirt and tan slacks. He was handsome, too, with dark bronze skin and a playful smile.

"I didn't mean to interrupt."

"You didn't," she lied as she stepped completely away from Carlos. "Are you from the painting company? I wasn't expecting you until tomorrow. Well, it doesn't matter, let me show you what you'll be working with." She was anxious to get away from Carlos, to get back to work, to what she was supposed to be doing.

"I'll gladly let you show me what you've been working with." He grinned at her, and she had to admit it was kind of sexy. Maybe it had been too long since she'd been with a man. Every guy she saw today she thought was good-looking. It had to be Carlos's fault. Her hormones hadn't been stable since she met him.

"Shut up, Elias."

"You know him?" Virginia looked back at Carlos, who had annoyance plastered all over his face.

"I more than know him. This is my little brother."

"Oh, good!" She smiled at the flirty younger man. He was built well, but differently from his brother. Shorter, thicker, more like a football player. "I was thinking that you were kind of gorgeous. I guess I was just seeing the family resemblance."

"Kind of gorgeous?" He placed his hands over his heart. "Girl, you wound me."

He was charming, too. She liked him immediately.

"Excuse me, ma'am." The movers were back. "Can you show us what you would like moved next?"

"Of course." She turned back to Elias. "I hope you're staying for a while. I'm going to make lunch."

Chapter 5

"Uh," Elias said as he closed the distance between them. "You want to tell me who that is?" He punched Carlos in the arm. "It's no wonder you don't mind being holed up here. You've got a woman with an ass that won't quit. When were you going to tell me about her?"

He punched Elias back a little harder than his brother had punched him. "There's nothing to tell. She's not some woman. She's the interior designer."

"Designer, my ass. You were about to kiss her."

Carlos shook his head even though he knew that was true. "We were just talking."

"With your lips inches from hers?"

"Yes." He didn't know why he was lying. If Elias had walked in on them two seconds later he would have been kissing her. The truth was, he had gone out of his room just to see her. He'd wanted to know what she was up to, especially when he'd heard the men's voices when he was on his way back from his gym. It was for her safety, he told himself. Hideaway Island was safe, but he didn't want anyone to think she was in this big house alone. "What the hell are you doing here anyway?"

"I came to see how you were. Obviously, you're doing pretty well."

"They're almost done." Virginia came back into the room smiling, as if she was happy for the company. She always seemed happy, even when there was nothing to be happy about. "What do you two want for lunch? I could grill up some hamburgers or some chicken. I've got all the stuff for jerk chicken and mango salsa. Or I could make you some pasta." She walked over the fridge and scanned its contents. "I can do some cheesy chicken and tomato pasta. It's really good."

"You don't have to cook. We can order in."

"Cook? Order in? Last time I was here you made us eat frozen pizza."

"I needed to get rid of it." Carlos shrugged. "Plus, you're not a guest. I don't have to impress you."

"I can cook. I like to cook." Virginia handed them both beers. "What sounded good to you, Elias?"

"So much about what you said sounded good." Carlos noticed the way Eli's eyes roamed her body. He couldn't blame him for looking at her that way, but he still wanted to knock him on his ass. She wore a sundress today. This one was short, in a coral color that looked so pretty against her brown skin. Her hair was loose today, her curls springing out in every direction. The first word that came to mind was *cute*, but she was more than cute. She was sexy. The way that she walked and talked and smiled was sexy, and the longer she was in his house the more he wanted her.

"Burgers sound good," Carlos answered for his brother.

"She wasn't asking you. She was asking me."

"It's my house. I decide." He looked back at Virginia. "We'll do cheeseburgers. I'll start the grill. You think you can make one of those fancy salads you like?"

"Of course. We'll eat by the pool, and while we do Elias can tell me all the embarrassing things about you that you never wanted anyone to know."

There were six painters there that morning. When she had called the island's only company, she'd asked if they were able to do such a big job. They'd assured her they could, that they would send out everybody they employed. And they had. She was now looking at six people in white overalls and hats, two of them well into their seventies and one who looked as if he should be in school that day. Virginia didn't know what to say when she saw the ragtag group, but they showed up with big smiles on their faces, ready to work and seeming very happy for the opportunity.

"Would you like some lemonade?" Virginia approached the elderly woman she had come to know as Cynthia with a tray. "I made it myself."

"Oh, thank you!" Cynthia smiled and put down her roller. "You're so wonderful to work for. Isn't she nice, Bobby?"

"Huh?" The elderly man stopped his painting and turned around.

"Never mind."

"What?"

"Never mind! Go back to work," she said loudly. "He can't hear. Deaf as a doorknob now and won't wear those fancy hearing aids we had to go all the way to Miami to get. Stubborn as a mule, but a good worker."

Virginia agreed. They all were good. She was relieved because painting was the first step in her design and she couldn't afford for it to be messed up. She had almost gone with a more experienced company that was off island, but Carlos had taken a chance on her so she was taking a chance on them.

There was a knock on the open door and she turned around to see a man standing there. He looked like a workman, in his paint-smeared T-shirt and jeans, but there was something ruggedly handsome about the man with the nut-brown skin.

"Hi. Can I help you?" She wasn't expecting any workmen today.

"Derek Patrick." He extended his hand.

"You're the guy who makes the furniture," she blurted out. "You're the mayor?" She was expecting an older man. Not this hunky guy before her.

His smile was bashful. "I am. I know I look like a homeless person, but I assure you, I'm the mayor of this fine island."

"It's great to meet you. I'm Virginia." Virginia shook his hand. "Your furniture is so beautiful. I was admiring it online and was hoping to use some of your pieces in the house."

"I would love for you to come by my workshop. I can custom make whatever you want."

"That would be amazing."

"Believe it or not, I didn't come here to drum up business. I came to thank Mr. Bradley for using local businesses. I encourage everyone to support our local economy."

"Don't thank him, thank me." She grinned. "I'm the one who hired everyone."

"I didn't hear that Mr. Bradley had gotten married. Congratulations."

"Oh, I'm not married to him. I'm just the interior designer."

"And that was just my way of finding out if you were single." He flashed a smile that would make a lesser woman's heart race. "Well, are you?"

"You're smooth, Mr. Mayor. I am single."

"I should be better behaved. I really would like to say hello to Mr. Bradley and welcome him to the neighborhood. But maybe you'll agree to have dinner with me one night."

"Maybe I will." Maybe she should. He was artistic and handsome, and maybe seeing him would take her mind off Carlos. She worked for him and he took up more room in her head than he should. Especially since the other day when she'd been just moments away from kissing him. "I'll go see if Carlos is around. Why don't you…" She looked around her, seeing if there was any place for him to make himself comfortable. "Grab a paintbrush and help out?" She motioned her head toward the kitchen. "Follow me and I'll set you up with some cookies and lemonade while you wait."

"I'm okay right here. I'll catch up with my friends."

She nodded and left him to see if Carlos was up for company. He had warned her that very first day not to bother him with anything. To handle things herself. And if it were anything else, she would have. She knocked at his bedroom door, knowing he was in there from the faint sound of the television. There was no answer, but she turned the knob and entered anyway. The room was huge and white. Completely white from the walls to the crumpled duvet on the huge bed. The only thing that broke it up was the chocolaty-brown wood floor. There was so much she could do with this room, but he didn't want her to touch it and she wasn't sure why. The sound of the television distracted her from her thoughts. There was a sitting area attached the bedroom, just like in her suite, only bigger, with a wall-size flat screen. A baseball game was on, and it took a moment for her to spot him sitting in the middle of the old black leather sofa.

"Carlos," she called to him. He didn't turn around, didn't give any sign that he heard her. She walked closer to him, and as she did she heard his name being said on the television. And then she saw him leap across the screen, his glove extended, going after a ball. He caught it, and for a brief second there was triumph on his face, but the triumph turned to pain when he landed and then he crumbled to the ground reaching for his ankle.

So that was it. The moment he'd got hurt. At first when she'd heard about the injury she hadn't thought much of it. Athletes got hurt all the time. He would go back to playing one day, but he had been out for a while and there were no signs of his going back. Baseball was what he did and he was no longer able to. Baseball was to him what painting was to her, except Virginia had exiled herself from the thing she loved. She walked closer. He still hadn't heard her; his eyes were glued to the TV, to the medics coming out on the field.

Why was he watching it? Why was he torturing himself? Who would want to watch the one thing that hurt them the most?

She picked up the remote from the side table and shut the television off. It was then he looked at her. And when he saw her in his space his eyes filled with anger, but just before that she saw sadness. That was the thing about him she hadn't been able to identify— there was an air of sadness around him that made her want to soothe it away.

"What the hell are you doing in here? I thought I

told you I didn't want to be bothered. In fact, your job depended on you not bothering me."

He was yelling, but it didn't concern her; she just kept walking closer to him, and when she was right in front of him she climbed onto his lap, straddling him. "Don't bark at me." She slid her hands over his cheeks and, pulling his face toward hers, she kissed him.

As soon as her lips touched his she knew that she had never experienced a kiss like it before. His lips were warm and smooth, full, just as she liked them. His body was hard and hot, and when she slid her tongue across the seam of his lips she felt something inside him switch on. He took control of the kiss then, taking her mouth with a vengeance, slipping his tongue deep inside as his hands slid under her dress to cup her behind.

Coherent thoughts flew out of her head; all she could do was feel. Feel his lips on hers and his hands on her body and herself become aroused. Dampness formed between her legs and suddenly she was too hot. She wanted to peel off her underwear, peel off her dress, peel off everything that was keeping her skin away from his.

He flipped them over so that she was on her back, his heavy body settling on top of hers, his hands reaching for her underwear.

"Damn it, Virginia." He lifted his lips from hers for just a second as he hooked his fingers into her panties.

It was then she came to her senses. Not because she had barely known him a week, not because he was her boss and she his employee, not even because there were six painters down stairs.

"Wait!" She put a hand on his shoulder, stopping him. "I came to tell you that the mayor is here. He wants to welcome you to the town and thank you for supporting the local economy."

"What?"

He was hard as a rock and pressed between her legs, making it really hard for her to think. "The mayor is here to see you. Now get off me. I'm not allowed to have sex with you anyway."

He got up, but the huge erection tenting his pants was distracting her. "You can make this disappear." He had caught her staring. She was embarrassed but she didn't look away. "I think since you're the one who created this problem, you're going to have to be the one to solve it," he said.

"The mayor is here!" She stood up, attempting to fix her clothes, hoping she didn't look as though she'd been about to have extremely hot sex.

Carlos stepped forward, grabbing her by the waist and pulling her into him. "Send him away." He kissed the curve of her neck, slow, wet, hot kisses that made her knees go weak.

"No sex. I can't." She smacked the back of his head.

He stepped away from her, looking annoyed. "Why not?"

"There's six painters down there, and in case I forgot to mention it, the mayor is also downstairs. Plus I make it a rule never to have sex in the middle of a workday. And I never, ever have sex with somebody I'm working for."

"Fine." He walked away from her and toward the door. "But if you think this discussion is over, you're wrong."

"Well, damn. I was going to come here tomorrow at the same time so we could start over, but you yelled at me and told me I wasn't supposed to bother you during the day." She thought about what she'd walked in on him watching, but didn't want to bring it up in that moment. Somehow seeing him wounded like that made her want him more than his deep sexy kisses. "I'd hate to disobey a direct order twice," she said as they went down the stairs and back into the great room.

"I'll allow you to disobey the order for that reason only." He grasped her arm, lightly running his thumb over her still-stimulated skin. "I thought you said the mayor was here."

"He is." She pointed to Derek, who had a roller in his hand and was painting while he chatted with Cynthia.

"That's him?"

"Derek?" She called to him. "I'm so sorry to keep you. My father would bust a gasket if he knew I put the mayor to work."

"I like to work." He grinned at her. "It's what I do." He walked over, extending his hand to Carlos. "It's nice to meet you. I just wanted to stop by and welcome you."

"Thank you. I appreciate that."

"I think I can speak for everyone here on Hideaway Island that we are honored that you have enough confidence in our workmanship to hire locally."

"You can thank Virginia for that. She's in charge of the house."

"I figured as much. Your interior designer is not only beautiful, but she's smart, too. You were lucky to find her."

"Yeah." Carlos wrapped his arm around her and pulled her close. "I am."

Chapter 6

Carlos pushed off the edge of his pool, propelling himself through the water. He had loved the water as a kid. His mother thought it was important for all of the Bradley kids to not only swim but to swim well.

He couldn't remember the last time he'd really swam, with his head under water and his body gliding through it. He had splashed in the ocean with his last girlfriend on the beaches on the coast of France, but it hadn't been anything like this. All he heard was the breeze and the water surge around him, the waves hitting the shore in the distance, the sereneness of being alone in nature. And for once his foot didn't hurt. There was no stiffness. No range-of-motion issues, no pain at all.

When his hand touched the other end of the pool, he flipped over and swam back, ready to do another lap, but when he lifted his head from the water he saw Virginia sitting on the new lawn furniture she'd had delivered that morning.

His blood heated when he saw her. She was wearing a long gray-and-black-striped dress; her hair was pulled up today in a bun on top of her head. He preferred it loose and wild with her ringlets bouncing, but she was beautiful no matter what.

"Hey." He stood up.

She smiled at him. She always smiled when she saw him. Her smile was a gift she probably gave to everyone, but it made him feel damn good when she gave it to him. "Hey, yourself."

He hadn't seen much of her the past few days. She was there. He knew when he went to bed at night that she slept one floor below him and all he had to do was walk down the stairs to get to her. But he didn't. Because he didn't want to do it that way. She had been working hard for him, always on the phone, always sketching something, always directing someone.

She was a professional, no matter how she'd acted the first time they'd spoken, and he could see why people liked to work with her. But working with her was the last thing he wanted to do. He wanted her in his bed, and ever since the day on his couch he'd been going around hurting because he wanted her so much.

"Do you like your new outdoor living room?" She leaned back on the couch. It was a dark brown wicker with blue cushions, the same as the rest of the chairs and loungers. It was sleek and comfortable looking at the same time.

"I do," he admitted. He hadn't paid much attention to the old stuff. He hadn't spent any time out here until she had arrived.

"I can't wait for the table to get here. I ordered a large one for big parties, but I got a little bistro set…"

She broke off, giving him a sleepy smile. "You don't care, do you?"

"No." But she did. She cared more about decorating his house than he had cared for anything in a long time. "You're off the clock, you know. No talk of paint or wall hangings or whatever you like to blab on about."

"I'll call Derek tomorrow. He loves to talk about furniture as much as I do."

He suppressed an eye roll at the mention of Derek's name. He was a nice guy who did good things, but he clearly had a thing for Virginia. She'd said she was just going to order some furniture from him, but Carlos knew that as soon as Derek got a shot at her he would take it. Carlos just had to make sure Derek never got his shot. "Come here."

To his surprise she got up without argument and came over to the edge of the pool, slipping her feet into the water. "Have you eaten yet?"

"No."

"I'm going to cook tonight. Will you eat with me?"

He grabbed one of her feet, stroking his thumb along her sole. She had bubble-gum-pink painted toenails that he found distracting and adorable. "You're tired. You don't have to cook. Let me order in."

"I think I can boil some pasta and grill up some shrimp without too much effort."

"You've been working hard all day. Let me take care of dinner."

"Oh." A mischievous smiled came across her lips. "You're going to cook tonight? I would like that."

"You really don't want to eat my cooking. Come in the water with me."

"I'm not wearing a bathing suit. Give me a few minutes to get mine."

He didn't want to wait a few minutes. He wanted her with him now. "You don't need a bathing suit."

She laughed. "I make it a rule not to go skinny-dipping with men I've known less than a month."

He tugged at the hem of her dress. "You don't have to be naked. Just go in what you have on under this."

"You want me to swim in my underwear? I think you just want to see what color my panties are."

He was curious, but more than that he wanted to see her body. See the thing he had been lusting over for the past two weeks. "It's no different from you wearing a bikini."

"I don't wear bikinis. I'm a one-piece kind of girl."

"Take off your bra and you'll only be in one piece. Get in the pool with me."

"Okay." She stood up, walking to the far side of the pool as she stripped off her dress.

Her body. It was full and curvy and delicious looking, but it wasn't slender, wasn't what some would consider perfect. It wasn't what he was used to. He had dated models and actresses for so long that he'd forgotten what a real woman looked like.

Right now this woman in her black bra and pink-and-white-polka-dot underwear turned him on more than anyone had in as long as he could remember. "You're walking in the wrong direction."

"No, I'm not." She took a running start and launched herself into the middle of the pool, splashing him in the process. "I haven't done that in years." She emerged from the water laughing.

"You splashed me." He went after her.

"That was the whole point." She swam away from him and he was surprised at how graceful she was in the water. But he was a good swimmer, too, and easily caught up to her, pinning her against the wall of the pool with his body. He had to suppress a moan, she felt so good.

"I see you're not one of those take-your-time, get-in-little-by-little people," he said to her.

"Life is too short." She wrapped her arms around him, resting her chin on his shoulder. "I always knew you were a beautiful man, but seeing you shirtless and wet just confirms for me how fine you are."

"You're the only person who openly tells me you like the way I look."

"Really?" She looked up at him. "It's true." She ran her hand up and down his back. "You're like a big, hard Greek statue. Like something my ex would have sculpted. Nobody in real life looks or feels this way."

"You sound annoyed."

"That you look perfect? It is annoying. It makes me feel as if I should stop eating brownies and start eating more kale."

"Eat brownies. You look—" he wrapped her legs around his waist, taking time to run his fingers down the backs of her thighs "—and feel amazing to me. You're beautiful, Virginia."

She kissed the spot where his shoulder and neck met. It was arousing, but more than that it was sweet. He couldn't remember the last time he'd been with somebody who was just sweet to him. "Thank you."

"Tell me about this sculptor boyfriend you had. Is he the same one who stole your cat?"

"Yes." She spoke into his shoulder. Her lips vibrated against his skin. "He had a beautiful, soulful spirit."

"But he dumped you by leaving a note your microwave."

"He hated confrontation. Breaking up with me in person would have been too hard for him."

"And it was easy for you to have someone you spent a long time with break up with you without having the decency to tell you face-to-face? He sounds like a punk ass to me."

"He wasn't. You would have to know him. He's sweet and sensitive. He used to paint my toenails while we watched TV, and he loved to go shopping with me. How many men would do that?"

"Hmm" was all he said, not wanting to give away what he was thinking.

"What?" She lifted her head off his shoulder and looked up at him with her eyes wide.

"Nothing." He shook his head.

"Something. What are you thinking?"

"Why did you break up?"

"I don't know. He said that I just wasn't the right one for him."

"Was there someone else?"

"No. At least, I don't think there was. We both worked from home. We were always together. Maybe he just got sick of me."

"You think he got sick of having sex with you?"

She opened her mouth to speak, but then shut it.

"What? Tell me."

"Sex wasn't important to Burcet."

"Burcet! What kind of name is that?"

"French. He was born in Morocco but spent his school years in France."

"So your Moroccan French sculptor boyfriend liked to paint your nails, go shopping with you, but didn't care about having sex with you. Let me guess, he liked to cuddle."

"Yes, he did. What are you trying to say?"

He shrugged. "I don't think I have to say it."

She gasped as it dawned on her. "Don't stereotype a man just because he likes to do things that a dumb jock like you would never think of doing. He was kind and he cared about me."

"And then he dumped you and stole your cat. Stop defending that asshole. You deserved better."

She rested her head on his shoulder again. "You're right. I moved here for him. He asked me to move here for him. Said he couldn't do it without me. So I picked up my life and left a job that I liked, one that I was good at, and moved across the country for him. And I supported him. Not just financially when he needed it, but I supported his dreams of being a sculptor when pretty much everyone else on the planet had given up on him. I said I liked every one of those oversize, pretentious pieces of crap he churned out. And the crazy thing is, I don't even think I loved him that much."

"Then, why did you do it?"

"I'm not sure. I guess it was for the sense of adventure. The feeling of not knowing how things would turn out. Asa and I grew up with such strict parents. Every single thing we did was scheduled and planned out. There was no spontaneity. So now that I'm an adult and I can do whatever I want, I make sure I do whatever I want."

"How's that working out for you?"

"Okay, I guess. If Burcet hadn't dumped me I would have never opened up my design firm. And if I didn't open my design firm, I wouldn't be on this beautiful island in this beautiful pool that overlooks the ocean with the man I'm going to tell my grandchildren about someday."

"Why would you tell your grandchildren about me?"

She looked up at him again, deeply into his eyes. "You can't be that humble. I may have thought you played for the Dolphins and had no idea when baseball season is, but even I know that you're a legend in the making and probably the most famous player in the game."

"I'm not a legend in the making. I can't play."

"You're hurt. You'll go back."

She sounded so sure of herself. He had missed an entire season. He had never missed a day since he was in little league. "What if I can't go back? Baseball is my job. I have no other skills. I didn't go to college. If I'm not a player, then what am I?"

She looked at him for a long moment, her expression turning thoughtful. "You're not just a player. You're a man. Your job doesn't define you. You know that, right? I've had a million jobs. None of them defined who I am."

"What if I don't know who I am?"

"Then, getting hurt was a blessing. Now you get to go on the adventure of finding out who you really are."

A blessing. He shook his head. After losing his father, getting hurt had been the worst thing that had ever happened to him. Baseball had been the thing that had bonded him and his father, and without the game it almost felt as if Carlos had lost him all over again.

The only thing that made life bearable now, that made it sort of livable, was Virginia's unexpected presence in it. Maybe it was her positive outlook on life. Maybe it was the way her soft, curvy body was pressed against his, but he felt lighter than he had in a long time.

"How does a man find himself?"

"Think of all the things you want and go after them.

You're luckier than most. You have more than most people could ever dream of."

"This money doesn't mean a damn thing to me. I want my father to be alive. I want to play ball again. I can't buy any of that."

"No. But you can't bring your father back and you can't get unhurt. Time doesn't go backward, only forward. Things don't mean possessions. Just think about what you want out of life, what will make you happy, and go get it."

The sun was just starting to set. All he could see was an orangey sky above them and the swaying palm trees around them, with the ocean serving as a backdrop to it all. Yet she was the most beautiful thing there, with her curls slipping from her bun and her large, soulful eyes staring at him.

"I want you," he said honestly, just before he kissed her. There was something about her that made kissing her feel more like an experience than anything else. It could be the way her body went soft, almost liquid, like the water they were in, or it could be the way her lips were hot and moist and pliant. Or the way she kissed him back, passionately, as if she was enjoying him just as much as he was her. He wanted her like he hadn't wanted anybody ever, and he had a sense that that feeling was never going to go away.

"Carlos." She broke the kiss. "I work for you. I just started working for you. I can't sleep with you."

"The sun is setting. You aren't working for me right now. Right now you are my friend."

Friend. It was the first time he had thought of her that way, but it was true. He had his teammates, his siblings, but he couldn't think of the last time he'd just had a friend.

"I don't have sex with my friends."

"Don't have sex with your friends. Just come to bed with me."

"No." She slid her hands up to his face and kissed him, softer than their last kiss, a little more slowly. She broke away, smiling gently at him, and then splashed him in the face and then swam off.

He laughed and chased after her. He had a feeling he was going to be chasing after her a lot.

Virginia checked on the painters' progress once more. There were only four of them today; the two oldest team members had taken a break from all the hard work. It was taking over a week to paint the massive great room—three days alone to apply the first coat to the stark white walls—but she was pleased with her color choice. *More cream than coffee.* Just that hint of brown in the white paint turned the room from a cold empty space to one that was much warmer and more inviting.

She was still looking through catalogs and scouring the internet for just the right pieces to put in there. Her instinct was to go completely homey, make the big room feel like a smaller space, feel like a place where a family could gather and enjoy, but the knowledge that Carlos's sister was getting married here made her pause. The public spaces of the house had to be more of a showpiece, something spectacular. Worthy of hosting a wedding full of important guests.

She wished Carlos would give her some guidance as to what he wanted, but every time she approached him he told her that he didn't care what she picked. As long as it was nice.

Nice? What a bland word. She pulled out her cell

phone and called Carlos. She wanted to let him know that she was heading to Derek's workshop in case he needed her. He never needed her. She rarely saw him until the sun was about to set.

"Why are you calling me?" he asked, answering his phone. "I'm upstairs."

"Calling you is a lot easier than walking up those stairs. Plus I didn't want to disturb you. You told me not to disturb you. Remember?"

"You can disturb me. Especially if we end up doing what we did the last time."

Her skin heated at the thought. She still went to bed thinking about that day, about how his heavy body had felt on top of hers, how his fingers had hooked into her underwear. She was trying to stay strong, stay professional, but she knew if she went into his room with his bed just a few feet away it would be much harder to say no to him. Saying no to him the other night while they'd been in the pool had almost killed her. She wanted him, but more than that she wanted to protect her heart. She fell in love too easily and had gotten hurt too many times. This time she was going to do things right. She was going to think of her career first.

"I just wanted to tell you that I was heading to Derek's workshop to pick out some furniture."

He was quiet for a long moment. So long that she thought they were disconnected.

"Hello?"

"I'm putting on my sneakers. I'll be down in a minute." He hung up before she had the chance to ask why. When Derek was there last week she'd thought she sensed some possessiveness on Carlos's part, but she might have been imagining it. He made it downstairs in record time. "Okay. Let's go."

"You're coming with me?"

"Yeah. I'll drive."

"Why are you coming with me?"

He blinked at her. "You're buying furniture for my house with my money. Do I need a reason to come?" He walked toward the door.

"Um…I guess not. You never seem very interested in what I'm doing."

"Maybe today I am. Maybe I just want to see his workshop, or maybe I want gelato and I want you to come with me. Let's go."

"Well. Okay, then."

He took the convertible instead of one of the two other new cars he kept in the garage and drove to the opposite side of the island with the top down. Derek had a small storefront shop in town, but he did most of his work out of his home.

They pulled up in front of a charming light blue house with a white picket fence around the yard. It was a large cottage with a beachy feel. A place that felt as if it belonged on Hideaway Island. It was the opposite of Carlos's house, which felt as though it was on an island all of its own.

"Are you going to help me pick out furniture while we're here?" she asked him as they walked up to the front door. "I really would like some of your input."

"If I see something I like, I'll let you know." He walked slightly ahead of her and knocked on Derek's door.

Virginia couldn't figure out what his endgame was. She'd never told him that Derek had asked her out. He couldn't be jealous. Derek was a great guy, but right now she only had room in her head for one man, and that man had bogarted his way into her shopping trip.

"Hey, Carlos." Derek's eyes went a little wide with surprise when he saw Carlos standing on his porch, but he genuinely smiled. "How are you, man? Good to see you. Hey, Virginia. Come in." He motioned them inside. Virginia noticed he was covered in sawdust and had goggles hanging around his neck.

There was a staircase directly in front of the door. To one side was a kitchen, and on the other side was his living room turned workroom, with some of the most beautiful pieces of handcrafted furniture she had ever seen.

"Wow." Virginia walked over to a bookcase that looked modern and yet a throwback to an earlier time. "This looks like something you would find in an old apothecary, or if you painted it black it would fit in any city apartment."

"That's what I was going for." Derek lovingly stroked the wood. "This is naturally weathered poplar. The handles and pulls are made from antique iron. This one has sold, but I can make you a new one and finish it in any color you like." He walked over to a larger unit with glass doors and black shelves. "I was thinking this would look amazing in the great room on the far wall. It's big enough not to get swallowed in that room."

"Oh, I agree."

"And this circular coffee table." He turned away and got on his knees in front of the low-lying table with intricate diamond-shaped cutouts. "You said that a couple of the bedrooms have sitting rooms. I was thinking about this for your room. Along with that midcentury-style tower bookshelf. We can paint it white and it would fit in with the color scheme you were talking about for that bedroom."

"I love that idea. Maybe you should come back over

to the house and go through all the rooms with me. I want a handcrafted piece in every one." She looked over at Carlos, who looked as though he'd rather be watching paint dry than be there with them. "What do you think?"

"Where do you do your mayoring?" he asked Derek. There was a little challenge in his voice that set Virginia's nerves on edge. "Is there a city hall? Shouldn't you be there?"

"Carlos!"

"What?" He shrugged, looking around the room, sizing it up. Sizing Derek up, mostly acting like an arrogant jock.

"No." Derek grinned. "It's okay. He pays taxes. He has every right to know where and how I work. I'm known as the mobile mayor. I always have my phone and laptop, and I keep office hours once a week. I'm not a sit-at-a-desk kind of person, but I think the way I do it has been effective so far."

"Yeah, okay." Carlos brushed off his answer and Virginia wanted to smack him. "I want a desk. You've got a desk here for me, Mr. Mayor? Nothing that needs to be custom-made that I'm going to have to wait a year for. I don't have time to wait for one of your custom pieces."

Derek nodded, keeping his face perfectly neutral. Virginia was having a harder time doing so. Heat crept up her neck, and not in a good way, either.

"How about this?" Derek showed them a large desk he had sitting in the corner. "I can finish it in a mahogany color. It's big enough for a man of your size and can easily fit in a corner or be the centerpiece of any office."

"Let's go with that. I want some shelves, too. You think you can handle that?"

"I think can handle anything you throw at me. I

manage to run this island and work full-time. Shelves shouldn't be a problem. I think Virginia would have no problem assisting me in that area."

Carlos looked at Virginia. "Let's start with the pieces we discussed already and we'll come back for more at another time. I'll be waiting for you in the car."

He walked out of the house then, leaving Virginia puzzled and a little embarrassed by his rude behavior. "I'm sorry about that." She turned to the mayor. "I think he's hungry."

"Yeah. For you. He's made that perfectly clear."

"But he has no right to..." She trailed off. He'd told her that he wanted her. There was no misunderstanding it.

"To claim you? You're a beautiful woman, and I think we might have a lot in common, but he's Carlos Bradley. I didn't want him to think he can stomp on me, because he can't. Though I do admire the man. I've been trying to play it cool, but I've got his jersey in my closet and a box of cereal with his face on it. I've been devastated that he can't play. All of Hammerhead fandom is mourning the loss of him."

"I'm mourning the loss of his manners. He acted like a teenage boy."

"All men act like teenage boys sometimes. I'll still jump off a roof if you let me. I'm not mad at Carlos. He sent over a very large check to help out some families that were in need on the island. He took away a lot of people's sleepless nights, including mine. If I really thought I had a chance with you I'd go after you in a heartbeat and not give a damn who that man is waiting outside. But I have a feeling that what you feel for him is just a little more than professional."

Derek was stable, attainable, available and normal.

Not to mention ruggedly handsome. She wished her heart raced at the sight of him the way it did for Carlos, the way it had since the first time she had met him. But she couldn't be with Carlos. It would complicate things, give her mother fodder when it all ended. And it would end. Because rich, beautiful guys like him never ended up with artsy girls like her. "I think your feelings might be off. Maybe you should think about asking me out sometime. Maybe you should think really hard about it."

"I will," he said, smiling in a way that most women probably found irresistible. She just found it pleasant.

"Let's get these pieces ordered. I'm not sure how much longer I can keep his royal highness waiting."

A few minutes later she walked outside to find Carlos leaning against the car. His arms were crossed over his massive chest. There was almost a cockiness to his posture. Heat curled in her belly, and it had nothing to do with the high temperature of the day. She was distracted by the way his biceps peeked from his T-shirt sleeves. How he seemed to take up more space than most men, even though they were outside.

He looked up at her, his eyes studying her with what she could only describe as possessiveness.

That annoyed the hell out of her.

"Take a walk with me," he said before she could say anything to him.

"Now?"

"Yes, now. I haven't seen this side of the island before." He grabbed her wrist and tugged her forward. The street was quiet, the only sound coming from the wind blowing through the palm trees. She forgot to be mad at him for a moment, she was so taken with the neighborhood. The houses were brightly colored and beautifully made. Shades of pink and blue and lavender greeted them as they traveled down the street.

And there were flowers everywhere, some of them wild, some of them maintained by the residents, but she knew she had never seen blooms like this, this big, this paintable. She touched a pink flower with sunny yellow tips. She had never seen anything like it. Pink, yellow, green in the center, tiny purple flecks where the seeds were. She could see this flower on canvas. With a bright green background and maybe some blue toward the edges to represent the sky.

"You like that?"

"It's gorgeous," she said, feeling awed. She had forgotten how engrossing nature could be. She had forgotten what it was like to be lost in a subject that she wanted to paint. She had forgotten the last time she wanted to paint.

Carlos picked the flower and placed it in Virginia's hair. "It's yours. You should always have beautiful things in your life."

She looked up at him, at his handsome face, at the sun that shone down on him, and she wanted to paint him, too. And then she remembered that she was mad at him for acting like a total jackass.

"Ouch." He jerked away from her. "Why the hell did you pinch me?"

"Why the hell did you act like a big macho ass in there?"

"I didn't." He rubbed his arm. "That hurt, damn it."

"Yes, you did. You were rude to Derek. In his home, I might add. And it was totally uncalled-for."

He shrugged and kept walking ahead, forcing her to go along with him. "Just because I asked him where he did his mayor thing doesn't mean I was rude. I bought a house here and am contributing a lot to the economy. I think I have a right to ask."

"But you don't have a right to be a jackass." The road was getting sandier as they walked down it and Virginia could feel the change in the air. It became damper, saltier. The ocean was never far away on this island, but she could tell they were getting near it. "You never care about what I'm buying for the house, but as soon as I said I was going to Derek's you rushed downstairs and had to accompany me."

"I still think I was well within my rights."

"Your right to be an ass."

"Enough with the name-calling. I just wanted to make sure you didn't order enough furniture to support this guy for the rest of his life. You bought enough today to get him through the rest of the year."

"It's for your house! He gave us a discount, and if you don't want his furniture all you had to do is say so."

He didn't respond, and she knew why as soon as they came to the end of the block. There were no more houses, just a small beach with an ancient-looking lighthouse on it. Virginia stopped in her tracks. She could see this on canvas with a vivid pink, orange and purple sky.

"His furniture is fine," Carlos said, distracting her from her thoughts. "We both know that's not what this is about."

"What?"

"I don't want him thinking he can go out with you."

She knew it. Derek had said as much, but hearing it from Carlos's mouth still jolted her. "But you're not my boyfriend, my husband or the boss of my body. I decide who I date. Not you. Derek is a nice guy. He's good-looking and we have a lot in common. Maybe I want to go out with him, and if I do there's nothing you can do about it."

"You're right." Before she could process his words he pulled her close and kissed her. There was power behind this kiss, and need, as though he was hungry for her. He buried his hands deep into her curls and his tongue deep into her mouth. Suddenly she forgot where they were. She felt the throb between her legs and the tightness in her nipples and she wanted to peel off every inch of clothes that separated them. And feel him inside her.

"You're right," he said, breaking the kiss and looking into her eyes. "But I want you. I want to be the only one who puts my hands on you, and that's not going to change anytime soon. Okay?"

He stepped away from her, turning around to strip off his shirt and causing her mouth to go dry. He kicked off his shoes into the sand. His shorts came down next, revealing his perfectly hard body. He wore gray boxer briefs that molded to his behind and made her want to cry out in appreciation.

"Wh-what are you doing?"

"I'm going swimming."

"Swimming?" It was the answer that made sense, but not the one she secretly wanted to hear. "Now?"

He turned to face her, an erection tenting his boxers. She stared at it. She couldn't help herself. She wanted to see what it looked like with nothing covering it, with no barriers.

"Are you going to skinny-dip?" she asked, her naughty side creeping out when she knew it was going to get her into trouble.

He shook his head, a crooked smiling playing on his lips. "See? That right there is why I want you." He walked away from her then and dived into the clear blue ocean.

She stood there watching him for a moment, just engrossed. Engrossed in the warm ocean air and the lushness of the tropical beach surroundings and in him. In watching his powerful body slide through the water.

She had two choices. Stay on the beach with her clothes on and out of trouble. Or go in the water with him and open up herself to a situation she might not be able to handle.

She kicked off her sandals and pulled her dress over her head. She was never one to travel the safe route.

Chapter 7

Carlos stood in the small upstairs bedroom that he had decided he was going to turn into his office. He had made the decision on a whim, really. A man like him, with a house like this, should have an office, should own a desk and a computer and some pens and stuff. Virginia had challenged him to think about what he wanted out of life, to find himself.

He didn't know where to begin. The only thing he had known for the past eighteen years was playing baseball.

The only thing he had thought about was how to get better. How to get his team to the playoffs. How to make his family proud.

But his mind was blank now. He couldn't see his life without baseball. He couldn't think of anything else. But he knew he was getting older, that even if he could go back next season he wouldn't be playing much longer. Maybe four more years, tops.

What then?

It was a question he had thought about, but it made his head throb. The only thing that came to the fore-front of his mind was an education.

He had never admitted it to anyone but he'd always wished he had a degree. Education had been impor-tant to his family. All his siblings had gone to college. Elias had gone to medical school. Carlos had so much, but he had gotten it using his body and not his mind. He thought about going back for a moment, but quickly pushed the thought out of his head.

He was too old. He hadn't picked up a book in years. He was pretty sure he had forgotten how to study. What if he couldn't keep up?

This was Virginia's fault. She made him think. She made him feel things he hadn't felt in a long time. And one of those things was jealousy. He knew full well he'd acted like an asshole. But something in his head screamed out *mine*.

His.

His decorator.

His friend.

His object of desire.

She was always in his thoughts. She wanted to keep things professional. She wanted to just be friends, but then she did things like swim in the ocean with him in nothing but her underwear. And she called him out on his shitty behavior and she teased him. And she kissed him like no one ever had.

She wanted to keep things professional?

They were already way past that.

He grabbed his cell phone and called her. It was after six. She should be done for the night, and he was tired of being in the house. He hadn't felt this restlessness

YOUR PARTICIPATION IS REQUESTED!

Dear Reader,

Since you are a lover of our books – we would like to get to know you!

Inside you will find a short Reader's Survey. Sharing your answers with us will help our editorial staff understand who you are and what activities you enjoy.

To thank you for your participation, we would like to send you 2 books and 2 gifts – **ABSOLUTELY FREE!**

Enjoy your gifts with our appreciation,

Pam Powers

**SEE INSIDE
FOR READER'S
SURVEY**

For Your Reading Pleasure...

We'll send you 2 books and 2 gifts
ABSOLUTELY FREE
just for completing our Reader's Survey!

YOUR READER'S SURVEY
"THANK YOU" FREE GIFTS INCLUDE:
▶ **2 FREE books**

▶ **2 lovely surprise gifts**

PLEASE FILL IN THE CIRCLES COMPLETELY TO RESPOND

1) What type of fiction books do you enjoy reading? (Check all that apply)
- ○ Suspense/Thrillers
- ○ Action/Adventure
- ○ Modern day Romances
- ○ Historical Romance
- ○ Humour
- ○ Paranormal Romance

2) What attracted you most to the last fiction book you purchased on impulse?
- ○ The Title
- ○ The Cover
- ○ The Author
- ○ The Story

3) What is usually the greatest influencer when you <u>plan</u> to buy a book?
- ○ Advertising
- ○ Referral
- ○ Book Review

4) How often do you access the internet?
- ○ Daily
- ○ Weekly
- ○ Monthly
- ○ Rarely or never.

5) How many NEW paperback fiction novels have you purchased in the past 3 months?
- ○ 0 - 2
- ○ 3 - 6
- ○ 7 or more

YES! I have completed the Reader's Survey. Please send me the 2 FREE books and 2 FREE gifts (gifts are worth about $10) for which I qualify. I understand that I am under no obligation to purchase any books, as explained on the back of this card.

168 XDL GJ3D/368 XDL GJ3E

FIRST NAME

LAST NAME

ADDRESS

APT.#

CITY

STATE/PROV.

ZIP/POSTAL CODE

since before she'd come into his life, and now he wanted to get outside and do something. He had the whole day when he could have gone out alone, but he didn't want to go anywhere by himself. He wanted to go out with her.

"Why are you calling me?" she asked as she answered her phone. "I'm downstairs." He grinned at her using his own words against him, but he couldn't help but to notice how tired she sounded.

"You okay?"

"Yeah. I've got a little bit of a headache that I can't seem to shake. I'm lying down right now."

"You want some aspirin?" He opened his bedroom door and made his way down the stairs.

"I took some earlier. It might be all the paint fumes doing me in. I kept a couple pieces of furniture you already had and repainted them today."

"By yourself?" He went into the refrigerator and pulled out some leftover roast chicken that they had and the potato salad she had made a couple days earlier. There was also a fresh loaf of French bread on the counter, just waiting to be slathered with butter. All this food was her doing. He couldn't remember the last time he had eaten so well. It was probably when he was a kid.

"Yes. I can do other things than pick paint colors and order things from catalogs."

He knew that to be true. He hadn't seen much of what she had done. But the little he had taken the time to notice was well done. It might have been crazy to hire her to decorate his house, but three weeks in he still didn't regret his decision. "Are you hungry?"

"I could eat, but I haven't been able to force myself out of this bed yet. I'll meet you in the kitchen in a few minutes."

"Don't bother. Stay in bed." Hanging up the phone,

he grabbed a bottle of wine out of the fridge and two glasses from the cabinet. He dumped all his findings on a tray and proceeded to her room. The door was open when he got there and she was sprawled out in the middle of her bed. Her dress was crumpled beneath her and had ridden up so her beautiful legs and thighs were exposed to him. She wore panties with blue hearts on them, and that aroused him far more than all the sexy, barely there lingerie he had seen over the years.

"When you told me to stay in bed, this was the last thing I expected."

"I thought we could have a little picnic."

She gifted him with one of her happy, sunny smiles that did more to him than any practiced seductress's gaze. "I think that sounds nice." She sat up, her hair even wilder than usual. "We can eat in the sitting area and throw open the patio doors and let some of the ocean air in."

"Why should we let the ocean air in when we could go to the ocean? The best part of being rich is having an ocean in your backyard."

"You want to have a picnic on the beach?"

He shrugged. "Why not? Grab a blanket."

She looked at him for a long moment before she turned to take one from the closet. "Okay. Let's go."

A warm breeze welcomed them as they stepped outside. They were quiet as they walked down the path that led to the beach, the only sounds coming from their feet shuffling in the sand. As the beach came into view his chest swelled a bit. This was all his. A private beach. An oceanfront mansion, more money than he knew what to do with. But sadness crept in there, too. He was alone here, when this place was meant for a family.

"Hope we can find a good spot," Virginia said as she put her hand over her eyes and looked around.

He shook his head and smiled at her lame joke. "You pick. Make sure it's away from kids. I don't want any sand kicked into my food."

"How about here?" She spread the blanket in front of the high beach grass and sat down. "Yes. This is the perfect spot." She patted the blanket beside her. "Come see." He put the tray down and sat next to her, so close that their arms touched. She leaned against him, as though it was natural. As though she had been leaning against him for a lifetime. "If I was going to paint this scene, this is where I was would capture it from."

"You paint?"

"I'm a painter. I mean, I was a painter. That's what my major was. I painted professionally for years before I became a designer. Didn't I tell you that?"

"No." He didn't know, but now that he did, he wasn't surprised. There was something about her, the way she looked at things, the way she studied things, took them in, simple things like flowers. Beautiful things. As if she was seeing them in a way no one else did.

"Well, I was. I sold a few, but the past couple of years I supported myself by doing restoration jobs and copies."

"Like forgeries?" he asked as he grabbed a plate and piled it with food for her.

"No." She shook her head. "I do a copy that's either bigger or smaller than the original. The client knows they are getting a copy. I signed my own name."

"But you don't do it anymore?"

"No. After Burcet left me, I took a long look at my life and decided I needed a change. Plus, I was spending more time on recreating someone else's masterpieces instead of trying to create my own. With interior design I can do that. Each house, each room is a blank canvas, so this is good for me."

"Hmm," he said softly, but he had a feeling that she missed painting.

"Did you know my most favorite thing in the world is cold chicken?" She picked up a drumstick and sank her teeth into it. "It's a little greasy, but the flavor settles that second day and somehow makes it even more excellent."

He reached for the bread, ripping off a hunk of it and handing to her before he assembled a simple chicken sandwich of his own. "Not every cold chicken is this good. You put something in it that takes it to another level."

"It's garlic-and-herb roasted. My mama's recipe. The only thing she can cook well."

"Your mother didn't cook much?"

"Nope." She leaned against him a little more as she bit into her bread. "She didn't have enough room in her head for practical things like cooking. It was too filled with theorems and numbers. She can make a mean roasted chicken, though, and a passable meat loaf. Other than that, my dad was mostly in charge of feeding us."

"Your father likes to cook?"

"No, but he'd rather eat his own cooking than whatever science experiment my mother put together. I took over the cooking duties when I was old enough."

"So if neither one of your parents liked to cook, how did you learn?"

"I just tried things out. Put together some things I thought would taste good. I also had an Italian boyfriend who taught me a lot. We spent a whole summer in Tuscany. I learned what good wine and good pasta was."

"Italian? Moroccan? You've got a thing for foreign men, don't you?"

"Accents. They used to turn me into a big pile of mushy mush."

"And now?" He switched to the Spanish he so rarely used. "Does it still have the same effect on you?"

She looked up at him, her eyes wide. "Well, that's an interesting little trick. Don't pull that one out too much. You might make women lose their minds when you roll your *R*s."

"I'm half Costa Rican. I can't cook any dishes from there, but my mother made sure we spoke Spanish. I think it was just so we would know what she was saying when she was angry with us."

"I always wished I spoke another language. I took six years of Spanish and the only thing I can manage to say is 'where is the library?'"

"Living in Miami, Spanish comes in handy. I guess my mother was preparing me for my time there since birth."

They fell silent for a few minutes while they ate. The sun was starting to set; the waves were crashing against the shore. A couple of seagulls flew above them. For once, Carlos was perfectly at peace. It seemed that he'd been searching for that feeling for years, only to find it with her.

Virginia set her plate aside, resting her head on his lap as she stretched out her long legs. She had to realize how dangerous that move was. He had been aroused since he'd walked into the room and seen her on the bed, her dress bunched up at her waist.

"I'm too tired to keep eating. I don't think that's ever happened before."

He stroked his hand over her thick curls, loving the

texture on his skin. "I don't think I've ever been too tired to eat."

"Hmm," she half moaned. "Maybe I'll go inside and rustle up dessert for us in a little while."

"Relax." He ran his thumb over the arch of her eyebrow. "You don't have to do everything all the time."

"I want to be useful."

"You do a lot. You do too much."

"I want to." She yawned. "I want to take care of you."

Those words made him pause, and he didn't know if it was sleepiness that had made her say them or if she really meant them. She wanted stay professional. She wanted him to stay away, but everything she was doing only brought him closer.

Virginia realized she must have fallen asleep as she felt Carlos shifting himself from beneath her. "I'm sorry." She scrambled to sit up. She hadn't meant to fall asleep. She'd only meant to rest her heavy eyes for a few moments, because no matter how tired she was, she hadn't wanted to miss anything.

How often did a girl get to dine on a secluded beach with the beautiful man who owned it? A man who was thoughtful enough to bring her dinner. A man who was gentle enough to stroke the hair out of her face.

"I didn't mean to fall asleep on you." But she had, because he was warm and comfortable and he made her feel safe.

"I didn't mind. I never mind having a beautiful woman in my lap." He smiled softly at her. "I was just going to suggest you go to bed. You look wiped out."

She grabbed his hand and pulled him down onto the blanket beside her. They were face-to-face, their bodies close but not touching, and it caused goose bumps to break out on her arms. "Not yet." She touched his arm, running her fingers down it. The combination of hard flesh under smooth skin was arousing. Everything about the night was arousing. She didn't know if it was the beach setting or him. Maybe it was a combination of both, but she knew she didn't want to be alone in that moment.

"Not yet?" The look in his eyes changed, as if he was trying to figure out what she was all about.

She hadn't even known herself what she was up to. Her mother's words were in the back of her head, serving as little taunts, just waiting for her to do something stupid. Sometimes she just wanted to be stupid.

He had kissed her that day at Derek's house. He had pulled her body close and kissed her, and she hadn't been able to stop thinking about his hands or his lips. The warmth of his hard body, his clean smell combined with the heady fragrance of sweet-scented ocean air.

"Stay here with me for a little while." She knew if they went back into the house she would come to her senses and go to her room alone. But as long as they were out here, on this beach, lying on a blanket in the sand, she could pretend it was all a dream. She could keep out her common sense and keep him with her like this for a little longer.

"Okay."

She could see the arousal in his eyes and she knew that it mirrored her own. She wasn't strong enough to tell him no. She didn't want to.

He gathered her into his arms, held her tightly against him. She loved the feeling, craved the closeness and his touch.

"You smell good." He ran his nose along the seam of her throat.

"That's because I aired myself out this morning."

"I appreciate that." He kissed her neck, just below her ear. "Take the day off tomorrow," he said as he ran his hand down her back, turning her into a bigger pile of mush.

"I can't." She sighed. "I booked this big job and I want to impress my boss."

"Your boss is already impressed with you. I'm sure of it. Take tomorrow off. I'm serious. I don't like that you're this exhausted. It's okay for you to rest."

"I'm not good at resting. Unless there's a fresh-smelling hard-bodied man to rest with me. Let's do something tomorrow."

"Like what?" He asked the question as if he really had no idea what the world could offer him outside his home. She was worried about him. It probably wasn't her place to be, but her mind still traveled back to the day she caught him watching footage of the moment he got hurt. He didn't think he had anything else to offer the world. He didn't think the world had anything to offer him besides baseball. That was wrong. There was so much out there for him. He just had to be willing to go out and grasp it.

"I don't know. Whatever you want to do. Something you've never done before. Something unexpected."

"Something unexpected, huh?" He kissed her shoulder.

"I'll make breakfast before we go. Pancakes, eggs, bacon. Maybe a little fresh fruit. Or should I make waffles instead? I love waffles."

"Hush. No more talk of breakfast."

She felt his hand wander beneath her dress to the small of her back. He stroked her there and a rush of tingles broke out along her skin, the same tingles that erupted every time he touched her like that. "Relax." He kissed her neck with soft, warm, sweet pecks, which shouldn't have been so erotic, but they were. She lifted her chin to give him more access and he rewarded her by sliding his lips across her throat, to that little spot that would have made her knees buckle if she were standing up.

"You make my heart race."

He rolled her onto her back. She expected to feel his body on top of her and his lips on her skin, but that didn't happen. He inched down the blanket, pulling up her dress until her belly and legs were completely exposed to him and to the nature around them. He sat back for a moment and just looked at her. There was appreciation in his eyes. She felt beautiful. That was a new experience for her. She felt beautiful and she didn't need words to feel that way, just his look.

"I'm not sure where to start," he said, more to himself than to her. But after a moment he seemed to decide and settled on her stomach. Her grabbed her hips and kissed her belly. She moistened then; never had she been intimate outdoors. It excited her to be here with him doing this.

"So soft." He kissed her again, this time hotter and wetter than before. His tongue flicked into her belly button and she flooded, the space between her legs becoming slick with want for him. "Your body... How I've missed a body like this."

His lifted his head and his gaze traveled to her thighs. She didn't think it was possible to be more turned on than she was in that moment, but he managed to do it just by looking at her, just by gently stroking his fingers up the curve of her inner thigh. "I want to take care of you this evening." He touched between her legs, his eyes darkening when he found her underwear wet. He rubbed her through the fabric, his fingers feeling good even though there was a barrier between him and her skin.

"Take them off," she moaned when he rubbed again.

"Don't be impatient," he said softly, his deep, smooth voice bringing her slightly closer to the edge. He slid her underwear off and trailed one finger down the center of her lips. She shuddered. He was taking his time. Oh, how she had wished for a man who liked to take his time with her. But now that she had him, she wanted him inside her as soon as possible. "You're supposed to be relaxing." He touched her slick folds, sliding his finger down the length of her wetness.

She gasped. She was so close to the edge already and he had barely touched her.

He found her spot, rubbing her in slow circles. She cried out his name, wanting more of him, wanting his lips on hers and his hands on her body and him on top of her pushing deep inside, but she couldn't get the words out. She couldn't do anything but experience his touch and the extreme pleasure it brought.

Climax struck her so hard it left her breathless, but that didn't stop Carlos. He kept stroking her through it, arousing her all over again. This time he slipped his fingers deep inside her, pumping in and out, causing another orgasm. It was more intense this time, causing her toes to curl and her back to come up off the blanket.

"Carlos…" She went to reach for him, but he didn't allow her to touch him; he just softly kissed her mouth once before he got up and walked away.

Virginia awoke to the sound of her cell phone ringing. Her thoughts turned to Carlos, who with one phone call had started them down a road from which she wasn't sure they could turn back. But it wasn't him. It was her mother. Of course it was her mother, the day after Virginia had done the thing she swore she wasn't going to do. Her mother probably had some kind of internal alarm programmed to go off whenever her children had done something they weren't supposed to do.

"Hello, Mother."

"It's after seven, dear. Are you still asleep? You sound as if you were asleep."

"I was asleep. How are you this morning?"

"I'm fine. Are you sick? Is that why you are still in bed? I thought if you did well on this job it could lead to other jobs and really establish your design career, since you don't want to come home and teach at one of the best universities in the world. And if you have a more stable career your father and I wouldn't have to worry about you every moment of every day."

"I could always go back to painting if I bomb at this."

"Stable, dear. Selling one painting a year and hoping the profits get you through isn't stable. You aren't getting any younger, Virginia. You have to start thinking about your future family."

"I know, mother. My eggs are drying up as we speak."

"Virginia." Her mother sighed heavily. "Don't be vulgar in the morning."

"I'm sorry. I know you can't stomach vulgarity before 9:00 a.m."

"No. Not at least until I've had my third cup of coffee."

And that right there was the reason Virginia loved her mother. She had a sense of humor under all her stuffiness. "Did you want something? Or did you just call to chat?"

"I wanted to see how your job was progressing, but

judging by the fact that you're still in bed, I gather I shouldn't inquire."

"He gave me the day off, Mom. That's why I'm lollygagging in bed at seven fifteen. On my days off I like to lie in bed till seven forty-five or so."

"So this football—"

"Baseball player," she corrected.

"Yes, baseball player. I looked him up. He doesn't seem to be into anything illegal. But he does seem to have a long line of scantily clad women in his past. A very long line. He's treating you well?"

She thought back to last night and a hot flush crossed her checks. "As far as bosses go, he's a decent one."

"If he tries to get fresh with you, you leave there. You don't have to take any kind of sexual harassment."

"Yes, Mom, I know."

"And if he does, or the job becomes too much for you, don't worry about getting a new one. I have a spot open for you here at the university. You would be such an effective educator. I've seen you with students. You seem to inform and entertain in a way that's rare."

"Why are you so convinced that I'm going to fail at this job?"

"I'm not. I'm just letting you know that you have options if this doesn't work out."

"You completely disregarded the fact that I'm actually good at this and I secured this huge job on my own. I've been running my business on my own for a year. I've never asked for your help."

"I didn't mean to make you upset, Virginia."

"But you did, and I have to go now, Mother. I'll speak to you later." She hung up and pulled the covers back over her head, just as she heard a knock at her door.

"You up?"

She peeked from under the covers to see Carlos standing in the doorway. "I'm up."

"You promised me breakfast and the beach today. Let's get moving."

Carlos couldn't take his eyes off Virginia as she sat in front of him in the small boat he had found in the garage. They were kayaking in the ocean. She had challenged him to do something that he had never done before, and this was one of those things. He had seen people in these skinny little boats, paddling out, and he had wondered what the allure was.

But now he was out in the middle of the ocean, with quiet all around him and the lush island scenery surrounding him, he understood. His mind had gone peacefully blank. For a little while there were just clear ocean and blue skies and a beautiful brown-skinned woman sitting in front of him.

She had tied her hair up. But there was one loose piece that was trailing down the back of her neck that was distracting. It was so alluring. He wanted to lean forward and kiss her there, but he couldn't. If he got up he might tip the kayak over.

Last night it had taken everything in his power not to take her. He had thought about her all night, as he'd laid hard in his bed. Even this morning when he went into her room, he wasn't sure if he could keep himself in check. She was so responsive to his touch, so giving of her body, so unself-conscious that it would have been easy for him to slip inside her, easy for him to spend the whole night with her. But for once he wanted to give something without receiving anything in return. It was the first time in his life he had ever felt that way about a woman.

But there was something wrong with her this morning. Something off. That easy happiness that usually floated around her was gone. As though her light had been dimmed. He had overheard just a snippet of her conversation before he walked into her room this morning, but he could tell she'd been talking to her mother.

They'd had breakfast together, and for other people it might have been the normal amount of conversation. But not for them. He missed her chatter. Most of his days were filled with silence, filled with his own thoughts. He hadn't realized how much the sound of her words had come to mean to him.

"Let's turn back," he said to her.

She glanced over her shoulder at him and nodded. "I didn't think I would like this, but I like it a lot."

"You could have said no when I brought up the idea," he said to her as they began to paddle back to shore.

"I rarely say no to trying new things. You never know what you're going to like."

She was right. He was discovering that more and more with each day he spent with her.

"There's…" She stopped paddling for a moment. "Are those horses?" She turned around to look at him. "There's a man with horses on your beach."

He just shrugged. "Let's go see what's up."

They were back to shore in a few minutes and he watched her climb out and run up to the two horses that were there.

He didn't get out for a minute. She was wearing a bright red bathing suit with strategically placed cutouts down the center. It was sexy, and the way it clung to her behind made him hard as a rock. He felt like a teenage boy when he was around her, barely able to control his body.

It took some kind of woman to do that to him.

He rose and went to her, watching her as she petted one of the horses. "She's a beauty, isn't she?" the owner, Tom Judith, said to Virginia. "Real sweet, won't give you any problems while you ride her." He looked at Carlos. "It's so nice to meet you in person, Mr. Bradley. We're honored that you've decided to make your home on the island. Everyone in town is really excited to have you here."

"Thank you. I appreciate that."

"I hope your tendon rupture is healing, because the team hasn't been the same without you. Baseball hasn't been the same without you."

There was a twinge in his gut at the words. For the past few hours he had forgotten that he had been hurt. He had forgotten that empty feeling that not being able to play left inside him. But now he was reminded that he was really nothing without it.

"Did you rent us horses for the day?" Virginia looped her arms around his neck and kissed his cheek, letting her lips linger there for a moment. "You're amazing," she said softly. "Just amazing the way you are right this moment."

He didn't know if she knew he needed to hear that, but he did. And it was nice to hear it from a woman who hadn't met him until after he'd left the game.

"You said, 'do something that you've never done before' and this is it." He looked back at Tom. "What are their names?"

"The mare is Kia. The gelding is Leroy. If you head west down the beach, you'll run into a nice trail that will take you into the state park. It's some nice scenery."

They put on their shorts and shoes, and a few minutes later they were both riding off down the beach toward the tropical forest.

"You look mighty fine sitting on that horse, sir," she said to him, giving him a sexy smile. "All you need is a cowboy hat. Maybe some assless chaps?"

"Why, thank you, ma'am." He tipped an imaginary hat to her. "I'm just trying to act cool up here on this horse. It wouldn't be manly of me to admit I don't know what the hell I'm doing."

"You know what you're doing. You are one of those people who is annoyingly good at everything they do. I, on the other hand, have trouble walking in a straight line."

"I'm not good at everything I do. I can't figure out what's been bothering you today." They came up to the tropical forest that bordered his property. The land was protected and could never be built on. It was the reason his nearest neighbors were miles away. It was the reason they felt so secluded.

"I'm fine," she said looking around her as they entered the park. There was a thick layer of leaves and branches above them, so thick that only tiny hints of the sky could be seen through them. "This place is amazing." He could hear the awe in her voice. He was a little awed himself as they traveled farther in. He had never considered himself a nature lover. He had spent his life outside on baseball fields because that was his job. But he had never done much else until he had come here.

There was kind of a magical hush that surrounded them. The sounds of birds chirping, dragonflies buzzing and horse hooves clopping on the earth beneath them made him feel almost as if they were exploring new land instead of traveling a well-worn trail that was just minutes from his house.

"You're quiet today."

She looked over to him "I'm enjoying my time with you."

"Tell me," he urged. He felt the heaviness about her and he didn't like it.

"My mother just drives me crazy. It happens."

"A lot?"

"I love my mother. She's brilliant and we get along fine when we aren't discussing my career or future."

"You seem as though you're doing pretty well for yourself to me."

"She's so sure I'm going to fail that she's secured me a teaching position at her university for when I do."

"Have you ever failed before?"

"She thinks my painting career was a failure. Any career that I choose that's not stable and steady is the wrong career to her. I get it. It's not the life she would have chosen for me, but I've never once gone to them for money. I never once got in the position where I couldn't take care of myself. I may not be who they wanted me to be, but who I am is pretty damn good, too." She shook her head. "Let's change the subject. I feel like I'm whining. I hate whiny people."

She wasn't whining. She was being honest and he liked that about her. "Why did you stop painting? Because of her?"

"I loved it." She shook her head. "I don't know. When I told her Burcet left me, she said, 'I told you so.' She said she knew it was going to happen. That he was all wrong for me. That he was just another poor choice I made. I thought maybe she was right. He was bad for me. Every man I have ever dated was bad for me, and I had this annoying habit of chasing them wherever they went. Giving up everything to follow some man's dream. I could do that with painting. But I thought if I had my own business with an office, that maybe I could break that cycle and prove to my mother and myself that I could be creative *and* practical. That I could put down roots on my own terms."

"You've given up painting to put down roots? That doesn't make sense to me, Gin."

"I painted some pictures for the Rosecove Inn because the owner knew my work. I hadn't found anything else I wanted to paint until I got here."

So *she* was the artist. He remembered the painting hanging in his room over the bed. A little brown girl sitting under a tree with her face turned up to the sun. He never noticed art, never stopped to take in paintings, but that had caught his attention. The way she had used color so vividly, the way she had painted the light to hit the child's face, the way she had captured the emotion of such a simple pleasure, had made him feel as if he could crawl into her work. It had made him remember what it felt like to sit outside as a kid and just soak in the sun.

"Let's go get you some paint."

"What?" She looked up at him, confused. "But we're horseback riding in the middle of this enchanted tropical forest. I don't want to go yet."

"No. Not yet." He didn't want their adventure to end yet, either. "I'll take you for a nice lunch, and then we'll go find some paint."

"You want to go into town?"

He didn't really. He didn't want to be faced with the questions and reminders of his vanishing career, but he would go today. For her. Because it was important for him to see her doing something she loved. "I want you to paint again."

* * *

"Is that Carlos Bradley?" Virginia heard somebody whisper as they browsed the only shop in town that had painting supplies.

She looked over at Carlos, who was busy fiddling with a toy robot, and felt sad for him. They'd had a good day, probably one of the best days of her life. He kept surprising her. The sunset picnic yesterday evening, then peaceful kayaking and horses that met them on the beach today. Not to mention the orgasm he'd given her, how he'd taken his time to make sure she was satisfied without asking for anything in return.

This wasn't her life. The past couple of days she'd felt as though she was in a dream that she didn't want to wake up from. Mostly. Little parts of real life had infiltrated. Her mother's call, but that she could handle, that she could ignore. But she couldn't ignore all the people who came up to him asking about his injury, expressing grief over his inability to play. She understood him better now. It would be like people asking her why she couldn't paint every time she left the house. A little reminder of the thing that affected him the most right now.

She could tell by the look on his face that he knew he had been recognized, but he pretended he didn't hear. He must be used to all the whispering by now.

"That is him. I'm going to go over there."

"Mom, don't."

"I have to."

Virginia left the limited oil paints and walked over to him, looping her arm through his. "You want to go?" She pressed her cheek to his arm.

"No," he said softly. "It's part of the job."

"But even you are entitled to a little off time."

"I've had it." He kissed her forehead. "Go pick out your paint."

"Excuse me, Mr. Bradley." A woman appearing to be in her sixties walked up with a young woman trailing behind her. "You don't know me, but I run the food pantry in town and I'm also the mayor's secretary and aunt. He wouldn't tell me who donated the money to help out our needy families, but I know it was you."

"No, ma'am." Carlos smiled shyly, and Virginia caught a glimpse of the man she saw on billboards and magazines. "It wasn't me. I don't know what you're talking about."

"My foot, it wasn't you." She rolled her eyes. "This isn't an island of rich people, honey. You're it. You're putting people to work. And you're minding your manners and that means I like you. And if I like you, I feed you. We want to throw you a little party at the community center. Next Saturday. Dress nice and come with an empty stomach. Bring your cute girlfriend, too."

She walked away before he had a chance to respond. He just shrugged and went back to fiddling with the robot.

Virginia guessed they were going to a party next week.

There were very few paint supplies on the island for serious painters like Virginia. The closest thing they had found was a beginner's oil-painting kit and some small canvases in the toy store. He bought them for her, even though she'd resisted and wanted to pay for them herself. He had never dated a woman who didn't seem at all interested in his money. Except for his last girlfriend, but she'd been too busy using him to propel her career. At the time he hadn't minded, chalking it all up to that kind of thing being a part of his life now, but it was different with Virginia.

And then he remembered it was different because he wasn't with her. They weren't dating. She worked for him.

Except for today. He wasn't her boss and she wasn't his employee. Today she was his friend, and as selfish as it was, he wanted more of her.

"The sun is starting to set," she said as she walked over to the glass doors that led out to the patio. "This day went by so fast." There was almost a sadness in her voice, as if she didn't want the day to end. He didn't want it to end yet, either.

He watched her as she stared out the window at the setting sun. She had showered and changed before they sat down to a fresh seafood dinner that he'd had delivered to the house. He should be used to looking at her by now, but he couldn't take his eyes off her. The curve of her neck, her chin, her shoulders. They were all places that he wanted to touch with his lips. Run his mouth over her soft skin, kiss her there.

"Today was a very good day for me, Carlos. It was one of my best days. Thank you for that."

He walked over to stand beside her, his need for her heavy within him. "You say it as if you'll never have another day like that. Tomorrow can be like today."

"Can you top horseback riding? What are you going to do next? Charter a hot-air balloon?

"I can if you want. I can do so much more."

He could whisk her away to a private island, but they were already surrounded by pristine beach and sand. He could take her to see the world, if she wanted. To Paris. To Buenos Aires. Anywhere her heart desired. He could give her things. Cars. Jewels. Whatever she wanted.

"I have to go back to work tomorrow."

But she didn't want any of that. She wanted him to respect her for what she could do.

"What if I don't want you to go back to working for me?" He pulled her into his arms and held her close. "What if I wanted to take you away? Name a place you've always wanted to go. Bora Bora? Australia? Africa? Nobody will know me there. No one will bother us." He kissed up the seam of her neck slowly, enjoying the way she went pliant in his arms. "Wherever you want, and we can leave tomorrow."

"I don't want to be your mistress," she said quietly, but with enough firmness in her voice so that he knew she wasn't going to take him up on his offer.

She slipped her hands under his T-shirt and rubbed his back as if to soothe his ego. No woman had ever turned him down before; no woman had ever rejected something he wanted to give. It stung a bit, but it made him want her even more, if that were possible. And now she was touching him. He wondered if he could make it to one of the bedrooms or if he was going lose control and strip her naked right there.

"A mistress is something you keep on the side. Somebody you use only when you want to. I'm not asking that of you."

She looked up at him. Staring him right in the eye. "What are you asking of me?"

It was a good question. It was one he didn't know the answer to.

Cupping the back of her neck, he covered her mouth with his own, kissing her deeply, the way he had thought about doing all day. Her mouth tasted sweet, like the wine they had been drinking after dinner.

"I'm not your type, you know," she said, pulling

away from him, but she didn't go far. She lifted his shirt, softly kissing his chest. "I'm ninety-nine percent sure that you only want me this much because you haven't gotten any in a while and I'm the only woman around."

"I could have any woman I want, but I only want you, Virginia Andersen." He pulled her into another kiss.

"Tomorrow we go back to the way it was before. You're my boss. I work for you. No more of this."

"No." He hiked up her dress, grabbing her behind, kneading her flesh between his fingers.

"Yes." She pulled away from him, unbuttoning his shorts, yanking them down until he was completely exposed to her. He had been hard since he'd first tasted her mouth, but when he saw her go down to her knees he became like steel. "It's my turn to do something for you." She kissed his head, rubbing it across her lips.

He hissed, surprised by her boldness, turned on by her touch. "Let me take you to bed."

"No." She kissed his shaft. "I want to do this just for you. Let me take care of you." She slid her wet, warm mouth around him and he knew he was a goner.

Chapter 8

The next morning Virginia was in the kitchen placing fruit in the blender for her morning smoothie when she heard heavy footsteps behind her. Her breath quickened, but she tried to control it. She never saw him this early in the morning. Sometimes she would hear him in his gym, but he never ventured into the kitchen when she was there.

Except for yesterday, when they had shared breakfast. Yesterday they had shared a lot more than just a couple of meals. She'd told him that things would have to go back to normal. That he would go back to being her boss and she his employee. It was the right thing to do. Right for her professionalism. Her career and her sanity. Having an affair with an athlete while working on his house was just the sort of thing she would do. It was the sort of thing her mother expected her to do. She had to prove her mother wrong.

She couldn't give into that temptation, even though Carlos made her body tingle with desire every time he came near her.

"Good morning." He wrapped his arms around her, pressing a kiss to her neck. He'd tried to get her to go to bed with him last night, but she'd refused. He hadn't pushed her on the subject and she was grateful for that because she knew she probably wouldn't have been able to tell him no more than once.

He had been so good to her yesterday. The horseback riding, the kayaking, listening to her while she talked. That alone would have made the day perfect. He'd taken her into town when she knew it made him uneasy, buying her paint, encouraging her to do what she loved again.

Four people had asked him about his injury yesterday. Four reminders of his loss, four expressions of concern, four disappointed faces when he couldn't give them good news. He hadn't had to go through that. He hadn't had to go into store after store in search of paint just for her. He had spent the entire day making sure she felt special. She'd just wanted to end the day making him happy. She'd wanted to give back to him before they returned to the way things were. But it had backfired because she had gone to bed unsatisfied, only wanting him more.

"Good morning," she returned his greeting as he kissed down the side of her throat. Her eyes drifted shut and she lost track of what she was going to say. "Want a smoothie?" She turned away from him and switched on the blender, hoping that would distract him.

"No." It didn't. He spun her in his arms and kissed the seam of her neck.

"A smoothie won't satisfy you? I can make you some

scrambled eggs," she said, her voice getting higher as her arousal grew. "I can put cheese in them. Onions. Whatever you want."

He removed his lips from her skin and looked into her eyes with those beautiful dark green ones he had. "You don't have to feed me, but I am hungry for something that only you can give."

He took her mouth then, in a slow, deep kiss that was so hot it curled her toes. She didn't want to stop him. Never had she been kissed like that, with such thoroughness, with such passion. This kiss made all the other kisses in her life invalid, incomparable to his. And she knew that for the rest of her life she would never know another man who could make her feel like this with just the touch of his lips.

"Carlos." She broke the kiss and cupped his face in her hands. "What the hell are you doing to me?" She kissed him this time, but with soft, sweeter pecks instead of deep kisses.

"It's not what I'm doing to you. It's what I want to do to you."

Resting her chin on his shoulder, she hugged him tightly. She didn't know what to say to that. But she knew she could fall in love with him. She knew she was the type of woman who could fall easily, but with him it would be different. With him she would fall harder, faster, deeper, irrevocably, and she wasn't sure her heart was strong enough for that. Because she knew he would get better, that whatever wound was inside him would heal and he would go back to his life as the future legend, the baseball player the world loved so much. And she would go back to her regular life. There would be no space in his life for her, and she was okay with that, but she knew it would hurt. She'd been disappointed when her last boyfriend had left, her pride wounded, but she wasn't hurt. She knew loving Carlos Bradley and then losing him would hurt.

The doorbell rang, alerting her that the painters were there, that her workday was starting. "I've got to go to work, Carlos."

He sighed. "Okay, Virginia. I'll see you later."

A week had gone by. A week of Virginia avoiding him, skirting away whenever he came near, a week of her only speaking of business matters, a week of him eating, sleeping and being without her, and he was sick of it. There were a couple of brief moments when he had caught her alone, caught her with her guard down, when she'd let him touch her, then kiss her until they both were breathless.

She wanted him just as much as he wanted her. There was no denying it. He could feel it in how she reacted to his kisses. Feel it in how she kissed him back, in how she looked at him and touched him. He had had chemistry with other women, but what he felt with her was more; it was deeper and it made him want her so badly he ached because of it. He hurt with need for her.

He went downstairs in search of her just as the sun was beginning to set. The workers usually left at five, and he knew that once they were gone she was his for the entire night. And she would be his. He didn't want to hear any more excuses. There was no denying it. No use in putting it off any longer.

What she had said to him stuck in his mind. That he only wanted her because she was the only one around, because she was convenient. But that wasn't true.

He had never been with a woman like her. Not one who looked like her. Or talked like her. Or acted like her.

But the truth was, no woman made him want her like this.

He found her in the kitchen icing a cake. She glanced up at him. "You wearing that tonight?"

He looked down at himself in his gray Hammerheads T-shirt and basketball shorts. "Is there a dress code for my own house that I don't know about?"

"No. But we are going to that party that Edith invited us to."

"Edith?"

"The woman we met in the store last week. The one who is throwing a party in your honor at the community center."

Shit.

"I forgot all about that." The little woman had forced the invitation on them. He didn't want to go. He hadn't planned on going, and that night Virginia had gone down on her knees before him and thoughts of that little party had drifted completely from his mind.

"You thought I was making this cake for you?"

"I got a little excited when I walked in here and saw, but then again, I have that reaction every time I come near you."

"Ooh." She smiled shyly at him. "You're a smooth player, aren't you?"

"You bring it out in me."

She shook her head, still smiling. "Go get dressed. We have to leave here in a half hour if we are going to be on time."

"I'm not going."

"What?" She dropped the spoon she was holding. "You have to go. This party is in your honor."

"I don't want to be honored. I specifically told Mr. Golden Boy Mayor that I didn't want anyone to know that I had given any money. Doesn't the Bible say that you're supposed to give to others without the expectation of reward or praise?"

"'Sound no trumpet before you,'" she said softly. "But they want to give you this party to give back to you. The whole island is going to be there. It will make them feel good."

The whole island?

He shook his head, the unease in his chest growing. He wasn't one of those people who liked being famous. He had been good at what he did, and the fame came along with that. Giving had been a part of his upbringing. He gave because it was the right thing to do.

"I don't want to be honored in front of all those people." He didn't want to be asked about his injury. He didn't want to be asked when he was going back. He didn't want to hear the disappointment about the team not making the playoffs this year. It made him feel as though it was all his fault. If he had watched the way he landed. If he had rested more after surgery. If he had just done something different he wouldn't be here; he wouldn't have to face a whole state's disappointment. "I'm not going."

"If you would have canceled at any point this past week I could understand, but now it's too late. We're supposed to be there soon and a lot of people went through a lot of trouble to do this for you."

"But I didn't ask them to!"

"No. You didn't. It's just a little party on a little island full of people who are grateful that they are going to have a home again. I know you don't want to face them. I know you don't want to be asked about your career or what's next, but the truth is, you can't hide out here forever. You can't avoid the future and you are going to have to figure out what happens if there is no baseball. The questions are never going to stop and you can't spend forever here living half a life and avoiding the people who made you who you are."

She stepped from behind the counter. She was right. He knew she was right, but it still made him mad as hell. Who was she to order him around? Who was she to point out what he already knew?

She stopped before him and wrapped her arms around his middle, diffusing some of his anger before he got the chance to say anything to her. "We only have to stay for an hour or so. Just a little while to let them know they haven't gone out of their way for nothing."

He said nothing, feeling his jaw clench so tightly it hurt.

"I'll owe you," she said softly. "Anything you want."

"Anything I want?" He grasped her chin and lifted it so that she could look into his eyes. "I'll go, but I'm collecting on my debt when we return and it's nonnegotiable."

There were dozens of cars at the community center when they arrived. Even Virginia hadn't realized how big a deal this was going to be until the day before, when she had overheard the tile guys talking about it. They were excited about the event, excited to see Carlos, because even though they worked in his house they never saw much of him. She should have warned him about it, about how this little party was turning into a bigger event for the island. But she couldn't bring herself to go to him, to put herself in his space, because she knew if she did, she would end up with his mouth on hers and his hands on her body. She was growing weaker when it came to him. It was bad enough that he plagued her thoughts, but when he was in the room with her she became magnetized, her body pulled toward his, and it would be too hard to break away from him without force.

But now she walked in with him, her arm looped with his, her body close to his tight one. He was angry. He was mad as hell at her, at the world, and he hadn't said a word to her since they left the house. But she had dressed for him. She hated to admit it, but she had put on a red dress that was just a little tighter and shorter than the rest of the ones she owned. She'd left her hair down and loose, putting product in it to stretch her curls and make them extra shiny. She wore heels, too. The highest ones she had brought with her that made her legs look sky-high and did things to her behind that she knew he would enjoy.

And he had enjoyed. When she met him in the foyer, his eyes had pored over her. They'd been hot. She'd seen the want in them, and the way he'd looked at her had made her nipples tighten with anticipation.

She'd promised him a favor. No questions asked, and she knew that favor would be her body. She wanted him, too. Her mother be damned. This job be damned. She knew that this night wasn't going to be easy for him. It was his first public appearance since he'd been told he couldn't play this season. She'd hoped that her short dress would be distracting. But she had hoped too much.

As soon as they walked in and saw the huge picture of Carlos sitting on an easel, she felt his body grow even tighter than before. "You look good in that picture," she told him. "Almost every picture I take my eyes are either crossed or closed, and I look as though something smells funny."

He looked down at her but didn't say anything.

They walked in farther, and she was relieved to see that everyone was in their best clothes. She had wanted to wear something special for him tonight, but she was glad to see she wasn't the only one in a dress while everyone else was in jeans. "You look handsome tonight, too. I don't think I've ever seen you in anything with buttons on it. Wasn't sure you owned anything like that."

"Please stop talking, Virginia."

She nodded, shutting her mouth as he led her into the building. There was a stage with a band on it. She recognized one of the painters as the drummer. They had decorated. White and gray and black balloons were everywhere. Hammerhead colors.

Food had been laid out on a long table in the back of the room. It looked like a potluck—mismatched plates and casserole dishes filled with finger foods and home-baked goods.

"I forgot the cake!" She looked up at him. "You should have reminded me."

Again he said nothing, and she saw Derek cross the room toward them. He was smiling, looking really good in a fitted blazer, button-down and jeans, but she could tell he was slightly embarrassed by it all.

"I'm sorry, man," he said to Carlos. "I told my aunt not to do this. She told me I wasn't the boss of her, which I am because I'm the mayor." He shook his head. "But I'm sorry. I warned everyone to keep their cool tonight. I half expected you not to show up. I know I might have run the other way, had I known what they were planning."

"Don't worry about it," Carlos said. There was no feeling in his voice, no angry look on his face, which might fool the rest of them, but she knew how unhappy he was.

"Miss Virginia." Derek turned his attention to her. "You look amazing tonight. I know a lot of men aren't going to be able to keep their eyes off the lady in the red dress."

"Why, thank you, sir. You're looking pretty good yourself."

"Where's the bar?" Carlos asked, and it was then she could hear the annoyance in his voice and she remembered that Carlos had marked her as his territory.

"It's a cash bar, sorry. Let me get your first drink. I'm sure people here will be buying them for you all night." He quickly walked away from them.

Then it started. A little boy came up to him. He was probably eight or nine years old, and there was awe and hope all over his face.

Carlos was pissed, but Virginia prayed that he would be kind to the boy. There was nothing worse than meeting your hero and being disappointed.

"Hello, sir," he said. "I'm in Little League just like you were, and I was wondering if I could shake your hand."

"Only if you can tell me the sixteenth president of the United States."

The boy scrunched his face. "Lincoln?"

Carlos extended his hand and smiled. "It's nice to meet you, son."

Thank God for children. That night Carlos surrounded himself with them. And there were plenty of them there. Lots of little ball players, both boys and girls, had taken all of his attention away from the adults. He was relieved. There was no pressure with the kids.

They were fun. Peppering him with questions, asking his advice. He enjoyed them. He was actually glad he had come. He worked with a lot of children's charities but he hadn't worked with a lot of kids. It was something he would like to do more often.

They ended up heading outside, where an impromptu game of baseball had broken out, and it was there that a twelve-year-old girl struck out every single kid and adult that she had pitched to. Imani Haymore had talent, but the island was so small that there wasn't a team at her level. She had to go off island and travel all over just to play, which was difficult for her parents and time consuming. Some college team had better scoop her up, but if they didn't, Carlos would pay for her to go to school. The kid was good. She would go far if somebody gave her the right push.

"Imani," he called to her after the game was done. She trotted over to him, still wearing the dress she had been in all evening.

"Yes, sir?"

"You're excellent. You struck everyone out."

"Not you. Now, that would have been something to tell people," she said with just a little bit of sass that made him like her even more.

"You know what my boys on the team would have said to me if I let a girl who isn't even a teenager yet strike me out? I had to get a hit."

She grinned at him. "I understand."

"Listen." He pulled a card out of his pocket. "Give this to your parents and have them call. I would like to discuss your future with them."

"Really?" She seemed surprised. "There's not even a softball team here."

"That's what I want to talk about. We've got to figure something out to keep you in shape."

"Thanks!"

She ran off and Carlos headed inside. They had been there for over two hours. It was enough. He'd had a good time with the kids, but it was enough for him and he was ready to go home. Virginia crossed his mind. She was wearing a red dress. He wanted to thank whoever had made that red dress, and thank her mother for giving her that body to put in that red dress. Because she looked that good tonight. All those soft curves and that lush body wrapped in one fiery package.

The band was playing a slow jam. The lights were dim, couples were dancing close together and that was when he saw Virginia with Derek, her arms looped around his neck, her lips curled into a wide smile. They looked as if they belonged together. As if they were together, but they weren't. And everything in his body screamed out that she was his.

But she wasn't. She didn't belong to him, and Derek was a good guy. He liked art. He liked to help people. They had a lot in common. He was stable and driven and knew what he wanted out of life. Carlos had money. He had fame. He had the power to get things done, but none of that was what Virginia wanted.

It made sense for someone like her to be with someone like Derek, but Carlos wasn't having it.

Because that little voice in his head kept screaming at him.

She's mine.

And I'm not going to let anyone else get her.

He walked over to them, his pressure up, blood pumping in his ears. He almost felt as though he was at bat in front of twenty thousand people, his mind fo-

cused on one thing. But instead of hitting a ball, it was
getting Virginia away from Derek.

"I think we've been busted," he heard Derek say
with a grin.

"We're not doing anything." Virginia frowned at up
at him.

Carlos took her arm and gently pulled her away. "I'm
ready to go."

"I was dancing with Derek."

"I know, and now you're not anymore." He kept his
voice low. He knew that all eyes were on them, and he
didn't want to create a scene, but he needed to get his
point across. "I thought we had an understanding, but I
guess I wasn't clear. Back off. You can have any woman
you want but her."

"Carlos," she hissed at him, but he never took his
eyes off Derek.

"Just leave her alone."

He turned away then, not waiting for a response, not
even caring if there was one. Virginia walked with him,
saying nothing. But the angry heat that was coming off
her burned his skin.

It didn't matter. He had gotten his point across, and
tonight he was really going to make her his.

Virginia couldn't even form words, she was so angry
with Carlos. The whole ride home she kept thinking
about how he'd come at them, charging like a big, angry
bull. At first she'd thought he was sexy. He looked big,
powerful and in charge. Hell, he *was* sexy. But she
wasn't his property or his girlfriend. She wasn't his
anything. But he was treating her as if she was. Even if
she was his girlfriend, he had no right to act like that.

Like a jackass.

Like a big macho idiot.

She got out of the car as soon as the wheels stopped and walked ahead of him into the house.

She wasn't used to men like him. Stubborn men who marked their territory and ran right over people.

He grabbed her hand, stopping her flight. "Where are you going?"

"To bed." She snatched her hand away from his. "Or more accurately to get the hell away from you."

"Why?"

"Why? Why? You may be a jock but you're not dumb, and if you don't know why I'm pissed you better call somebody to find out."

"I didn't do anything wrong," he said, so calmly and surely that she believed he thought that.

"You embarrassed me. You bullied Derek in the town he runs. You walked out on the party without thanking or saying goodbye to anyone. You were a self-centered jackass."

"I want you," he said simply. "I want to be with you and I don't want anyone else thinking they can have you." He stepped closer to her and gripped her shoulders. "When I think about somebody else touching you or kissing you it makes me crazy. I can't stop thinking about you. And nothing you do or say is going to stop me from wanting you."

The words hit her right in the chest. Right in her heart. She was trying to fight off the effects but it was hard. It was so damn hard when he had just said to her the sweetest thing anyone could have said.

"It's doesn't make it okay, you know. It doesn't."

He closed the gap between them, bringing his body in contact with hers. It was all heat and hardness. The contact made her heart race and her knees weak. It made her breath short as she struggled for something to say to him.

"I…"

The words died on her lips when Carlos leaned in and kissed her. She relented and let herself be kissed. There was no stopping what was going to happen tonight. She didn't want to stop what was going to happen tonight, even if she could.

He broke the kiss and looked down at her, his chest heaving slightly. "Your room or mine?"

"Mine." She sighed. "I promised you I would before we left."

He rested his forehead against hers and sighed. "I would never hold you to that. I would never make you do something you didn't want to do."

She looped her arms around his neck. Being with him was not something she wanted to do, it was something she needed to do. She couldn't resist the powerful pull between them anymore. "I want you. Just you. Only you. Still, you didn't have to be such an ass."

"I'm sorry." He looked at her for a long moment before he kissed her again. There had always been a spark between them, a heavy attraction that she couldn't deny. But when he kissed her this time, it lit something inside her. It made her hot, literally, as if her skin was burning up and only his touch could soothe it.

"Let's go." He took her hand and together they rushed to her bedroom. He pushed the door closed behind them and for a moment they stood staring at each other.

His eyes swept up her body, giving her goose bumps. "What are you thinking?" she asked.

"Two things. Having a house this big sucks in a situation like this. Bedrooms are too far."

"And the other?"

"You look so good, I don't know where to start."

His words made her breathless. She was experiencing more than arousal. It was excitement. She was excited to be loved by this man. "I know what I'd do."

"What?" A small smile played around his lips.

"Start from the top and work my way down."

"I think I'll do that."

He walked behind her and unzipped her dress. She felt his breath on her skin and her nipples became painfully tight. He kissed her, her shoulders, her back, the skin that went down her spine, as his fingers undid her bra. He pushed her bra and dress off all at once, leaving her in just her underwear.

He cupped her breasts, squeezing them slightly, his lips traveling to her neck, giving her the most scorching of kisses.

"Carlos…"

He brushed his thumbs over her nipples, sending ripples of sensation throughout her body. She didn't need this. She didn't need foreplay. She didn't need him to take his time. She was ready for him. She spun in his arms and kissed him hard, grabbing the waistband of his pants, unbuttoning them to slip her hand inside. He was hard already, but she couldn't resist stroking up and down his long, thick length.

"No." He gently pushed her away. "My turn to be in charge." He lifted her up over his shoulder and carried her to her bed, gently dropping her when he got there.

"I'm ready." She held out her arms to him. "Come here."

"You're ready, but I'm not yet."

"Take off your clothes. I need to see you."

He nodded, pulling his shirt over his head. "Take off your shoes."

She had forgotten she had them on, but she quickly took them off and discarded them, waiting to see what he was going to do next. He took some condoms out of his pocket and handed them to her.

"You always walk around with these?"

"No. Only tonight. I always want you, but I need you tonight."

His words were sweet. It made her want him even more. "Come here." She reached for him but he pushed her down on the bed. He grabbed her panties, slipping them off in one smooth move. "Still my turn." He pushed his head between her legs, kissing up her inner thigh, his lips getting closer and closer to her to mound. He kissed her there, closemouthed, then he parted her, licking deep inside. She gripped the comforter, biting down on her lower lip to keep from crying out as his tongue worked.

She was so close to climax, but she didn't want to yet. Not without him. Pushing his head away, she got off the bed to finish undressing him. She rubbed her body against his, loving the way her nipples felt as they scraped across his muscular chest.

"Why are you rushing me?" He brought his lips down on top of hers.

"You started it," she said between kisses. "I'm going to finish it the way I like." She grabbed one of the condoms off the bed and opened it. "Lie down," she ordered.

He did, resting his hands behind his head. She knelt between his legs, cupping his sac in her hand, pressing kisses to it while she rolled the condom on. He groaned. She loved that. She loved when he made any sound that showed his pleasure. Making him feel good made her feel great, like a woman. It was definitely something she'd been missing in her last relationship.

She climbed on top of him, straddling him, and he grinned. But the lust in his eyes was unmistakable.

"I think you're amazing."

"You should." She grasped his manhood in her hands and slid it over her lower lips. He hissed, baring his teeth. She didn't think it was possible, but seeing him like that turned her on even more. She rose over him and placed him inside her, loving the way it felt to finally have his thickness filling her.

She placed her hands on his chest and rose up again, slowly, until he was almost out of her, before she bore down again.

He growled but she maintained her slow pace, needing to feel every inch of him on every slide. He grabbed her hips, trying to take control, but she wouldn't let him. She bent her head, flicking her tongue across his nipple as she rode. That pushed him over the edge.

He flipped her over, pinning her to the bed. "You're too good." He pushed into her harder, deeper, faster. Her thoughts evaporated and her senses took over.

His lips sought hers and kissed deeply as he pumped into her. She couldn't be passive. She kissed him back, pushed against him. She wanted to give to him as much as he gave to her. She clenched herself around him as she felt her climax starting to build.

"Damn it," he cursed. He seemed to lose control, then he pumped into her harder, making her even slicker than before. She couldn't hold off any longer, and orgasm struck her. She cried out his name, digging her fingers into his hard back. He followed soon after her, slamming into her one last time before he came.

He collapsed on top of her, his breathing heavy but

his body completely relaxed. She kissed his forehead, stroking his back and shoulders, not wanting this closeness to end yet.

"I'm crushing you." He moved to lift himself off her, but she held on to him.

"You're not."

He rolled over to his side, taking her with him. "I'm not going anywhere yet. I don't think I can walk right now." He buried his face in her throat and kissed her there. "You're amazing. Has anybody ever told you that?"

"No, but a lady always like a compliment."

They lay there for a long time, saying nothing. His fingers played in her hair. Part of her was waiting for him to get antsy, to make an excuse to go upstairs and retreat to his space now that he had gotten what he wanted. But he didn't seem as though he was in any hurry to move. In fact, he seemed to be making himself more comfortable. He buried his fingers in her curls and rested his lips on her forehead. It was nice. It felt good. It felt like something she could get used to.

"I hate to be the girl to ask after we had such good sex, but you're still going to respect me in the morning, right? We're still going to be…friends?" She didn't want her mother to be right. She didn't want to be used for her body. She didn't want to be used, period. She hated that there was so much doubt there. She hated that she just couldn't enjoy the moment.

"Yes." He slid his hand up her hip. "Friends who have sex…a lot."

"You still want to have sex with me?" she asked, laughing.

He looked at her seriously. "Did you think this was a onetime thing?"

"I don't know." She felt silly, not like a sexually experienced woman but more like a teenage girl with her first crush. "I'm half expecting a gift basket at my door in the morning."

He exhaled, shaking his head. "You're never going to let me live that down. I promise you, I'll never give anybody another gift basket as long as I live."

"No. I would still like one. I like presents. Just preferably not when you're done with me."

"Okay." He grinned. "We'll decide when this isn't right for us anymore. If you don't want me here, if you don't want to do this anymore, just tell me to bounce and I'll go. But I don't want to go just yet."

She nodded.

"Can I stay tonight?" He gave her a long, deep, slow kiss that made her melt into the mattress.

"That's cheating," she said when he lifted his lips. "You can't kiss a girl like that and expect her to give a clearheaded answer."

"I don't want you to give me a clearheaded answer." He touched her breast, stroking her nipple to hardness. "I just want you to say yes."

"Yes." She pulled him down on top of her. "I couldn't send you away tonight if I wanted to."

Chapter 9

A month later Carlos ventured outside his house in search of Virginia. The World Series was on, and at first he had planned to sit and watch it, but as soon as he'd turned it on a pit had formed in his stomach. He should have been there.

He was supposed to have been there last year. He had been once before, but they had lost. Last year had been his chance to win. He knew he was getting older, that his time left to play was limited. He had wanted to go out on top instead of just going back. Maybe there was a slight bit of hope. Maybe he could go back next season. His heel was feeling better. He had his range of motion back. He felt strong.

But he also felt conflicted. The thing he had missed the most for so long, he didn't miss so much anymore. In fact, there were days he didn't think about it at all. It was strange. He'd thought he might be able to watch the game, but it reminded him too much of what he had missed.

But right now he was missing Virginia. She had been working hard on the house and he could see that, little by little, it was coming together. He still didn't know what her final plan was, but he knew that the house felt different. It didn't feel so empty anymore. And it was starting to feel like home.

The cars were in the garage, so he knew she hadn't left, but she wasn't by the pool or anywhere in the house.

The breeze kicked up as he walked down to the beach, the weather turning slightly cooler now that they were well into fall. He spotted her a little ways down. She had her easel set up, a palette in her hand. He hadn't seen her paint once since he had gotten her the set. He had all but forgotten about it, but he was glad to see that she hadn't.

"Hey." He walked up behind her, wrapping his arms around her waist and pressing his lips to her bare shoulder.

"Hey," she said, not taking her eyes off her work but relaxing just a little into his arms.

They had been sleeping together for a month now. At first he had thought things might be different between them, awkward even, but they weren't. If anything, they had grown more comfortable with each other. Not like two people in a relationship would, but more like very good friends. He couldn't think of the last time he'd had a friendship like this.

He also couldn't remember the last time he had spent so much time with a person. He went to bed with her every night and woke up with her every morning. Some nights they didn't even have sex, they just talked until they fell asleep. And he was okay with that. He was okay just being with her, and he had never felt that way about another woman before.

"Your painting is beautiful."

"No, it's not. I don't have the right colors or tools to really capture what I want. Even if I did, I'm afraid it would be nothing more than average."

He disagreed. She had captured the sun setting on the beach perfectly, from the way the light hit the water to the way the waves lapped the shore. He was no expert, but he found her work beautiful.

"Why are you so hard on yourself?"

"I'm not hard on myself. I'm honest with myself. There's a difference."

"No, you're bossy. How the hell are you going to tell me what I find beautiful? Your painting is beautiful. I want to hang it up."

She put down her palette and paintbrush and turned in his arms. "Are you going to hang it on your refrigerator and show all your friends?"

"No, I'm going to hang it in my bedroom."

"But you sleep every night in mine, so you don't have to see it. You should really let me decorate it, by the way. I could make it so nice for you."

He ignored her comment about decorating his bedroom. It was fine as it was. "I'll hang it in my office over my desk."

"Why did you need a desk? What do you do in your room all day?"

He hesitated before he told her, afraid of what she was going to say. "I used to sleep all day, but now I'm going to school."

"To school?"

"I never went to college. You asked me what I wanted out of life, and I've always wanted an education, so I decided to take classes. I'm taking two courses online. One in communications and one in sociology."

"Carlos!" Her face lit up as she hugged him. "That's amazing. I'm so proud of you."

"It's just a couple of classes," he said, but he closed his eyes and hugged her back. Her words meant a lot. Nobody had told them they were proud of him in a very long time. He knew his family was; that went without saying. But the last person to tell him had been his father. The day he closed on this house. Right before he died.

"It's not just a couple of classes, Carlos. We both know that. I'm so happy for you."

"Hold your happiness off for now. We don't know if I'm going to pass yet."

"I know you'll pass."

"You sound so sure."

"I am sure." She kissed him softly. "I know you."

He nodded. He was starting to think she was the only one who did.

A few mornings later Virginia's cell phone rang. She looked at it on her nightstand and sighed. It was after 7:00 a.m. and she should probably be up already, but Carlos still lay there, sleeping. His arm was wrapped protectively around her, his face buried in the back of her neck. She had never slept like this with another man before. She liked her space, but she didn't mind the closeness with Carlos. In fact, it was hard to get up in the mornings because she knew it was going to be a long time before she could crawl back into bed with him.

His hand moved beneath her nightgown and cupped her behind. "You going to answer that?" His deep voice was rumbly, sleepy, sexy. She was immediately turned on.

"You going to give me a reason to ignore it?"

His hand curved over her breast as the phone stopped ringing. He lightly pinched her nipple, causing a tiny bit of pain. He shifted himself and she could feel his erection pressed against her backside.

"Yes." He hiked up her nightgown and touched her between her legs. "I'll give you multiple reasons if you let me."

"Mmm," she moaned, as he stroked her to complete arousal, but then her phone rang again. And she placed her hand over his, causing him to stop. "Maybe I should just see who it is."

"Okay," he said with a heavy sigh.

She reached for her phone, seeing that it was Willa calling. Willa never called this early. "I've got to take this." She answered the phone. "Hello?"

"Hey, girl. Are you okay?"

"Yes. I'm fine. Why?"

Carlos rose over her with a mischievous look in his eyes and pulled down the straps of her nightgown, revealing her breasts. She tried to swat at him, but he caught her hand and pinned it behind her head.

"I haven't heard from you in weeks, that's why!"

"What are you talking about? I email you every day." Carlos bent his head and flicked his tongue across her nipple, which caused her to lose her train of thought for a moment. "I—I texted you last night before I went to bed. Why are you up so early anyway? I don't usually get you before noon."

"I haven't gone to bed yet. Stayed up all night writing. Had a breakthrough on the book. Now back to you. I wanted to hear your voice. We haven't spoken in forever. I wanted to make sure that that baseball player you're working for doesn't have you locked up in a basement somewhere, making the rest of us think you're alive by sending emails from your account."

Carlos pulled her nipple into his mouth, lightly sucking on it in a way that always drove her wild. "Stop," she hissed at him, but he ignored her. It felt too good. It was making her forget her thoughts.

"Virginia!"

"What? Sorry. You need to stop thinking that everyone is a serial killer. I'm fine."

"So this Bradley guy is treating you okay?"

He switched breasts, laving her, turning her on to the point she almost dropped the phone. She smacked the back of his head. "This Bradley guy is a pain in my behind, but probably one of the better clients I've had."

"So spill it. Tell me all about him. Tell me the dirt."

"Yeah," he whispered before he gave her a short but scorching kiss. "Tell her all the dirt."

"What dirt?" she asked both of them.

"Does he have a parade of panty-dropping women going through there? Is he a drinker? A gambler? Does he refer to himself in the third person?"

"What? No."

"Tell me something about him," Willa said sounding frustrated. "Your emails have been very unforthcoming about him."

Carlos positioned himself between her legs and wrapped her thighs around him. He was pressed against her opening and she was throbbing, ready for his invasion.

"Can I call you back later?"

"Why can't you talk to me about him now?"

"Because he's right here, Wils."

"I'm right here," he whispered in her ear, and he rubbed his length against her. "I'm right here waiting to bury myself inside you." He pulled her lobe between his teeth and she had to bite her lips to suppress a moan.

"Right there?" Willa asked. "It's seven fifteen in the morning. He's with you?" She was quiet for a moment. "Virginia Rose Andersen! He's in your bed, isn't he? You little hussy."

"Shut up!"

Carlos took the phone from her. "Hello, Willa. Virginia is going to have to call you back later. I'm sure she'll tell you everything." He hung up and tossed her phone aside.

"Did you just hang up on my best friend?"

"Yes." He kissed her, sucking her tongue into his mouth in a kiss so heated it almost brought her to the edge. "Apologize for me later." He started the slow slide inside her and it felt different, more intense, and she couldn't help but cry out. And she couldn't help but to admit that she was starting to fall in love with him.

Carlos walked out onto his patio with a blanket in his hands. It never really got cold on the small island even in mid-November, but he had been chilly the past few days. Virginia had been sitting outside on the patio for the past hour. She had taken to finishing up her work out there. Probably to get away from the noise of the workmen.

He found her sitting on the outdoor sofa, her laptop on her thighs, catalogs plastered with sticky notes on the coffee table before her. "I thought you might be cold." He wrapped the blanket around her shoulders and saw that she was looking at flights on her computer.

His chest felt tight for a moment, but he tried to ignore the feeling as he sat down beside her.

"Thank you for the blanket. I was going to go in but I like sitting out here."

"You're welcome." He motioned to her computer screen. "You going somewhere?"

"Yeah. I'm going home."

He fell silent for a moment. He'd known this would end eventually, but he hadn't been expecting it to end now, not yet. "You're quitting on me?"

She blinked at him. "The house is not done yet. I've never quit in the middle of a job."

"Then, why are you going home?"

"For Thanksgiving. My brother got off from work. My father isn't traveling. My family is all going to be there for the first time in a few years."

"Oh. Of course." That made sense. Of course she was going home to see her family. He didn't know why he didn't think of it before. He knew the holiday was just around the corner. He'd just talked about it with Elias. His brother had mentioned he would be working a double shift that day.

He hadn't thought the idea of Virginia leaving him would shake him so much. She was his friend, somebody he really enjoyed being with, but she was still his decorator. She was really there just to do a job. She was going to go home when she was done and he would go on with his life.

He'd known going in that they were temporary.

Hadn't he?

Maybe after she was done he would go back to Miami, too. Get on with his life. He had been comfortable here, hidden away with her. But maybe he was too comfortable. Maybe he was healed enough. Maybe it was time he reconnected with the man he used to be.

"What's wrong?" She set her hand on his knee.

"Nothing," he said, meaning to be truthful, but he couldn't bring himself to tell her what was going on in his mind.

Carlos's twin siblings had arrived unexpectedly for a visit. Virginia had been barefoot when she answered the door, her hair standing wildly all over her head, blue spray paint from the bookshelf she was refurbishing on her clothes and skin. Having met Elias before, she was only a little self-conscious to be seen looking like a big hot mess. It was his baby sister, Ava, who made her feel out of place.

Ava was an exotic stunner. A knockout by anyone's standards, with big dark eyes, long black hair, beautiful bronze-colored skin and a slender but curvy figure that most women would kill for. She was dressed to the nines in a designer shift dress and shoes.

And was sporting one of the biggest diamonds Virginia had ever seen. It was no wonder Carlos wanted the house redone for her wedding. She looked as though she was the type of woman who wouldn't settle for anything less than perfection.

"I've got freshly made strawberry lemonade," Virginia told the twins as she led them to the kitchen. "We have hummus and crackers, and a little bit of chicken salad left."

"Virginia." Elias wrapped his arm around her. "Always the hostess. You don't have to go out of your way for us. My brother will probably throw a piece of meat on the floor and make us fight over it."

"Not while I'm here, he won't. When I finish this job, it might be another story. Please sit." She motioned to the island's stools. "You can have something to drink while I go see where Carlos is. Is he expecting you?"

"No," they both said in unison.

"We always just show up to check on him," Ava said.

"Does he need checking up on?" Virginia poured them icy glasses of lemonade.

"I think so," Ava said, taking a sip and looking at Virginia over the glass as if sizing her up. "Elias doesn't. He said now that you're here we are relieved of duty, but I told him you're the interior designer, not his caretaker. Though judging by the way you keep the fridge stocked, I think you were well needed. This lemonade is amazing, by the way."

"What are you two doing here?" Carlos came into the room with a textbook in hand. He had a big exam coming up and he had been studying for days. She was really proud of him. It took a lot of bravery to go back to school almost twenty years since he'd last seen a classroom. She wasn't sure she could take it. But he was doing well and treating it as seriously as he did baseball.

"We came to see you. You never come to see us," Ava said, getting up to hug him.

"I shouldn't have to come see you. I bought the town house you live in and the car you drive. The least you could do is come see me." He tossed his textbook down on the counter and hugged his sister back.

"I'm not complaining," Elias said. "I came to see Virginia anyway. I was hoping she had some of those cookies she made the last time I was here." He picked up the book Carlos had just set down. *"Understanding Change in the Social World?"* Elias looked up at him. "What is this?"

Carlos looked at him as if he didn't know what to say. Virginia was surprised that he hadn't told his family he had gone back to school.

"It's nothing. Don't worry about it."

"This is a textbook." Elias narrowed his eyes. "You wouldn't be walking around with this for no reason."

"He's taking a couple of classes," Virginia said.

"Virginia, don't."

"Why?" She walked around the counter and touched his arm. "There's no shame in that."

"You're taking classes? Like college classes? And getting graded? Why the hell would you do that?" Elias asked.

Carlos shot Virginia a look and she knew he wasn't happy that she'd told, but she didn't understand why. "Why did you want to become a surgeon?" she asked Elias.

"To help people, but, Carlos…"

"You could have helped people by being a teacher or a social worker or feeding people in a homeless shelter. If you'd hated school and education you would have never become a surgeon. Have you considered that maybe your brother wants to learn a little more?"

"Nope." Elias shook his head. "Carlos has everything a man could want or need. And he's going back to play baseball. Most people get a degree so they can get a good job and lead a comfortable life. I don't see why a man who is doing what he loves needs to go back to school. It's a waste of time and money."

"And I don't see why you just can't be supportive. If he bought a hundred-thousand-dollar car you would be supportive. Why not with this?"

"Look." Elias raised his hands in a defensive posture. "I'm not being unsupportive. Carlos can do whatever he wants to do. I just don't see the point."

"You are being unsupportive because instead of saying 'that's great' and 'I'm proud of you,' you questioned him."

"That's enough!" Carlos slammed his fist down on the counter. "Both of you. I'll go back to school if I want to, Eli. You always act so damn superior to everyone because you're going to be a surgeon, but you aren't the only one in the family who has any brains."

"I know. I…"

"Shut up," Carlos snapped. "I paid for your schooling. Your books. Your supplies. Obviously I value education, because if I didn't, you would be like millions of other people with student debt loan so high that you'd never be able to climb out of it."

"I know," Elias said, subdued. "I'm grateful for it."

"You damn well better be, and you better know it's not your place to question what I do with my time or my money." Carlos looked at Virginia. "I need to speak to you in private." He walked out of the room not waiting for her response.

She followed him into the great room and looked into his angry face.

"I'm—"

"You're not talking now. I am. It wasn't your business or your place to tell them that I was going back to school. It was mine."

"I don't see what the big deal is. It's nothing shameful. It's a good thing and I'm proud of you."

"But it's my family and my business and you need to remember your place in it."

Her place.

It stung to hear that. But it was true. She had forgotten that she was just an employee to him. That he was paying her for her services. The "going to bed with him every night and waking up with him every morning" thing must have scrambled her brains. Made her think that she was more to him than a warm body to have sex with.

She'd been fooled into thinking that she was more than an employee, more than a friend. But how quickly that changed when she got into his business.

"I'm sorry." She held her head high. "It won't happen again."

He nodded and they walked back into the kitchen. Ava and Elias had matching unreadable looks on their faces.

She turned away from them, not wanting to face them and took out more snacks. "It was nice meeting you, Ava. Good to see you again, Elias. I need to get back to work."

"What?" Carlos said. "I was going to take everyone out to lunch."

"Have a nice time." She brushed past him, but he grabbed her shoulder and spun her around.

"You don't get to touch me." She pushed his hand away.

"But, Gin…"

"I had forgotten my place. I need to get back to it now, Mr. Bradley."

"You're an idiot," Ava said to him. "A big, stupid, macho idiot. I don't even want to look at you right now."

"What?" he asked, even though he'd known he had screwed up as soon as he'd seen hurt cross Virginia's face. He didn't have an excuse, either, but his going back to school was something he had wanted to keep private. He was unsure of how he would do, unsure if he would excel, and if he didn't, he hadn't wanted anyone to know about his failure.

"I really like her," Ava said, getting up. "She's good for you, and any woman who will defend you like that is somebody you should want to keep around. I thought you were smart for going back to school, but you're a dumbass if you told her she had better know her place. Daddy would have never said that to Mommy and you should have known better than to say it to her."

She walked out. Going in the same direction as Virginia.

"You're my big brother, Carlos." Elias looked up at him. "And I owe you so much. You had the right to put me in my place, but your girl…" He shook his head.

"I feel like shit already, but she's not my…" He stopped speaking. He slept in her bed every night, spent every day with her. She meant a lot to him. But what the hell were they? What *was* her place in his life?

What they had was more than a fling.

"I see the way you look at her, the way she looks at you. You going to tell me that there's nothing going on between you two?"

"She's my friend."

"A friend you're in love with."

"What?" Elias's statement caused a physical reaction in him. It was like a kick in the gut. In love? He had never been in love before. "No."

"No? You look at her as if you're in love with her."

Carlos shook his head. He couldn't describe what he felt for Virginia. He cared a lot for her, but love? The thought had never entered his mind.

"Maybe it's not my business whether you love her or not. But if you don't apologize, you're going to lose her, and you can't afford to lose somebody that good in your life."

Later that evening Virginia heard heavy footsteps as she sat in the dining room, putting the finishing touches on a sketch of the room that would become Carlos's office. She stiffened slightly but didn't lift her head or acknowledge him. There was nothing to say. She did like his little sister, though. She had apologized for him and called him everything but a child of God. Though that was not the reason Virginia liked her. She was down-to-earth; despite the expensive clothing and perfectly placed hair, she was lovely to be around. Virginia had spent the part of the afternoon showing her the progress she had made with the house. And when Ava had left to go to lunch with her brothers, she had given Virginia her number and hugged her.

"You're good for him," she'd said into Virginia's ear.

Virginia disagreed. She worked for him.

"Hey," Carlos said as he came to stand behind her.

"Hello." She tried to focus on her sketch but couldn't because he was standing so close to her. She could feel the heat of him, smell his clean scent. He had a way of affecting her senses, scrambling her thoughts into mush and making her common sense flee.

"I need to talk to you."

"Am I taking up too much space here? I can go into my room to work if this is bothering you."

"Virginia…" He pulled out the chair beside her and sat down. But he still didn't give her any space; he sat too close to her. His big body was touching hers. "I missed you at lunch today. I wished you would have come."

"I was working. I work for you, remember? I can't afford any more distractions."

"I'm sorry." He set his lips on her shoulder. "I was an asshole. You should be mad at me. There's no excuse for what I said and I'm sorry for it."

She had nothing to say. She was feeling dangerously

close to tears. This was the exact opposite of what she wanted. This was what her mother had warned her about—getting too emotional. Growing too attached. Thinking with her heart instead of her head.

"I'm sorry," he said again. "My sister is mad at me and my brother thinks I'm a fool. They both think I'm lucky to have you in my life right now."

She shut her eyes, feeling her chest grow heavy.

"Say something."

"I don't want to talk to you."

"Say something besides that."

"I thought I was your friend, but you treated me like an employee, which I am. But you can't have it both ways."

"You're my friend."

"Friends speak their minds and friends tell each other the truth. Friends are proud of each other. I'm proud of you and I'm not sorry about that, and I don't regret telling your family that, because you should be proud of yourself, Carlos. You're not just a bank account or a baseball player. You don't have to put yourself in any one box, and you don't have to be ashamed of anything that you do."

"I don't know why I didn't tell them. I guess I was going to wait until it was over, because if I failed no one would know but you and me."

She shook her head in confusion. "Why do you keep thinking you're going to fail? You haven't failed at anything yet."

"Baseball made things easier for me. I didn't have to study that hard in school. Teachers passed me. The principals looked the other way. Having me play for them was good for the school. All I had to do was show up.

That's why I wasn't sure I could do this. I was afraid I was dumb."

She laughed. "Everybody is a little dumb in some way. You're not dumb, Carlos. Don't ever think of yourself that way."

He cupped her face in his hands, slowly stroking his thumbs over her cheeks. "I'm the one who is trying to apologize to you. You're not supposed to be making me feel better about me. I really am sorry, Gin." He gently kissed her lips. "I don't like that I hurt you."

She believed him. She looked into his dark green eyes and she believed him. "I know, but you only get one of those. If you hurt me again, I'll be out of here so fast your head will spin."

Virginia looked up at Carlos as he stared blankly at the television. It was one of the rare times she spent time in his room. He had always come to her. There had never been any discussion about it. But tonight she was here, huddled under a blanket with him, their bodies touching, as close as two people could physically get, but she almost felt alone. As if he was someplace else, far away. He had been that way for a few days now. Quiet. A little distant. Maybe it was her. Maybe she was the one who was distant. They had made up. She had forgiven him, but was doubting herself. Questioning if still being with him, even casually, was the right thing to do.

Rationally she knew it wasn't, but there was something about him that wouldn't allow her to break away.

Somewhere along the way she had stumbled headfirst into love with him.

Of course she had. It was something she would do.

But at least she was smart enough to know that she couldn't stay in love with him forever.

The house was coming along nicely. A few more weeks, maybe a month, and she would be done. She had taken inspiration from catalogs but bought pieces locally and refurbished some things people wanted to get rid of on the island. No waiting fourteen months for lamps. She had no plans of extending this any longer than needed.

Maybe Thanksgiving would be a good time to break things off. They would be away from each other then. She hadn't been away from him one night since she'd walked in his front door in late August. Maybe they needed some space from each other. Maybe she needed some time away from him. She was leaving for New Jersey the day after tomorrow. It would be the perfect time. She could think clearly. Be away from him, from his kisses, from his touch, from the way he looked at her as though she was the only woman in the world.

The news came on; the police drama she had barely been paying attention to was over. "Record-breaking storm to hit the northeast could affect travel plans for the holidays."

"What?" Her heart dropped. She was going home to see her brother. She wanted to talk to him. When nobody else in the world understood her, he did.

"It looks as though it's going to clear up Thanksgiving night," Carlos said, grabbing her hand and stroking his thumb across her knuckles. "You can fly out the day after."

"This messes with your plans, too. Are you still going to your sister's?"

"No. I was just going to stay here."

"Why? You have family that wants to see you."

"My sister Christina has a big dinner with her husband's family and I'd rather shove a fork in my eye than spend a holiday with Ava's prig of a fiancé. Besides, my mother is right. Thanksgiving isn't the same without my father. It was his favorite holiday and it's just not the same."

There it was again. That sadness in his voice, that grief that made her heart hurt. "How was it?"

"It was…fun. My dad had taken to deep-frying a turkey and grilling a rack of ribs his past couple years with us. We'd play cards and board games, and he would always cheat. It just seems wrong to celebrate without him. It's been five years. I thought I would be over it by now."

She cupped his face in her hands and looked into his eyes. "You never get over losing someone so close to you. I didn't know your father, but I know he wouldn't want you still mourning his loss instead of celebrating his life on his favorite holiday. He wouldn't want you to be alone. He wouldn't want you to avoid celebrating or being thankful for all the things you do have."

He wrapped his arms around her tightly, resting his chin on her shoulder. "I've always worked hard, but I really threw myself into the game when he died and it got us to the World Series. Then it was all gone…just like that. Just like he died. A heart attack. Here one day. Gone the next. Losing baseball made me feel as though I had lost him all over again."

"He's not here with you on Earth, but you didn't lose him. Maybe it's a good thing the storm of the century has changed our plans. Maybe we are meant to celebrate his life instead."

Chapter 10

"Where are we going?" Carlos asked Virginia as she walked past the pool and onto the path that led to the beach. She was holding a dish of candied yams and he followed her with a turkey.

One that was far too big for just two people. She had been cooking all day. After she found out that her flight had been canceled due to the weather, she'd made him go grocery shopping with her, first asking him all the things his father had liked to eat—even if they weren't Thanksgiving related.

She had made him call his mother for her recipe for *sopa de mariscos*, a tomato-based seafood soup. And they had picked up board games and a deck of cards, any and everything that reminded him of his father.

And now she was leading him out to the beach at sunset, underneath the pretty orange and purple sky. She looked back at him and smiled, not answering his question about where they were going.

"I love turkey, Gin. But I do not want to eat it sitting in the sand."

"You won't have to."

It was then he saw the table sitting on the little pier. As he got closer he saw that it had a white tablecloth and was set beautifully with candles, the rest of the food laid out and waiting for them.

There were few times in his life when he'd had no idea what to say, no way to put into words what he was feeling.

"How did you manage this?" She had been bouncing around the house all day, preparing more of a feast than a meal just for two. He'd stayed with her while she had. She'd told him that he didn't have to, but he'd stayed to cook with her, peeling apples for the pie and forming biscuits from the dough she had handmade. He had never cooked with a woman before, never had the desire to, but he liked to with her. He sat there and listened while she talked about everything, about nothing, and it made his day better. Made it feel fuller. Made him less sad than he had been every holiday since his father died.

"Can't tell you all my secrets." She grinned back at him. "I know this is a long way to go for dinner, but I thought this might be nice."

It was nice. It was beautiful and more than he expected. It was more than he deserved. She'd gone out of her way for him, even though he had hurt her. She did so much for him and he couldn't think of one thing he did for her. But there wasn't anything he could think of doing that could equal this. He wanted to make it up to her. He wanted to do something special, just for her.

"Carve the turkey." She handed him the knife before she turned away to put food on their plates.

She set one in front of him, piled high with traditional Thanksgiving fare and all his father's favorites. There were cheese grits and hush puppies right along with his stuffing and honey ham. She had done too much.

He served her some turkey, and when he was done she sat on the side of the table closest to him instead of across from him. They both were quiet. He had been quiet for a few days now. He knew it. But there had been so much going on in his head. So many thoughts since Eli had accused him of loving her.

No, not just loving her. He did love her; there was no doubt about it. But his brother had accused him of being *in* love, and that was a different story. A deeper, more telling story.

What did it mean to be in love?

His life was at a crossroads. He didn't know where he was going next or how he was going to get there; he was just taking things one day at a time. And part of him was afraid he wasn't good enough for her.

Most of his adult relationships had been the opposite. He'd had everything to offer and nothing to gain, but this time it was different. He wasn't really sure of the man he was anymore. How could he be the man for her?

"I think we should say what we are grateful for." She reached over and grasped his hand. "It's what we do in my family every year. I'll go first." She shut her eyes.

Damn, she was beautiful. Pretty in pink with her wild hair blowing in the breeze and a serene look on her face.

"I am thankful that I can see and hear and smell and taste and touch. It's because of those things that I can enjoy life's small pleasures. I am thankful for this beach and this island and this sunset because it made me want to paint again. And I am thankful for Carlos. Because of him, I have had a new wonderful life experience."

Her gratitude made him want to smile, but he didn't. He was too busy thinking about what he should say. He was thankful for her, because she made him get out of bed and enjoy things. Enjoy life. She made him smile and she surprised him. She made him feel happiness. *Happiness* wasn't a word he normally had in his vocabulary. Even before he'd lost baseball, even before his father had passed, his life had been good but he had been only content. He had never felt the stirrings of happiness until this beautiful woman with her unconventional ways had changed that for him.

"It's your turn."

"Ditto."

"You can't say ditto." She laughed.

"What you said sounded good."

"Carlos…this is Thanksgiving. Give thanks, silly."

"Thank you." He leaned over and kissed her softly. He lifted his head slightly when he was done to find her eyes had gone half closed and her expression was soft and dreamy. "I'm thankful for you. I'm going to miss you when you go tomorrow." It was selfish. He hadn't wanted her to leave for Thanksgiving. He wanted to keep her here with him on this little island where the outside world didn't matter. But he knew he couldn't do that forever. He knew he couldn't deprive her of the family she had been missing so much.

"Come with me," she said.

"What?"

"Come home with me tomorrow."

He wanted to say no. He didn't want to meet her parents. He didn't want to think about her life outside here, but he said, "Okay." He said it before his brain could catch up to his mouth.

"Okay?" She smiled. "Thank you."

He didn't know why she was thanking him. She had just saved him from missing her.

Snow on Thanksgiving. Virginia was completely unprepared for the blanket of white that covered her parents' neighborhood. Not because it was still fall and they didn't normally see the first snow until well into December. But because she had been in Miami for so long and spent last night walking on the beach in a sundress and bare feet. She wasn't used to cold. She wasn't used to wearing close-toed shoes. Some days she didn't wear shoes at all and now she was walking up to her parents' house hearing the crunch of snow under her feet. She also wasn't used to walking up to her parents' house with a man she had brought home for them to meet.

She saw that her father's car was parked in the driveway, covered with snow. It wasn't like him to leave it like that. He was usually the first one on the block out with his snowblower, clearing everything, making sure that the outside of their house looked tidy.

"I don't think I've seen snow in almost twenty years," Carlos said from behind her. He picked some up in his gloved hand and just looked at it, a smile spreading across his face. "It's the sparkling kind of snow. This is Ava's favorite kind. She used to say that God had dumped glitter in it."

Even though she was nervous about him being there, she was glad he was with her. He seemed to find the cold air and winter scenery refreshing. "That's sweet, but if I never saw snow again I would be perfectly happy."

"That's because you're warm-blooded." He came behind her then, dropping some snow down the collar of her coat.

She screeched as the cold stuff dripped down her back. He laughed, his dark green eyes twinkling.

Damn, he was sexy.

"Oh, you think you're going to get away with that?" She grabbed a handful of snow and tossed it right in his face.

"Oh, you're playing dirty?" He took a few steps back, quickly made a snowball, wound up and threw it at her, hitting her smack dab in the middle of her chest.

She launched herself at him, knocking him backward into the snow. She should have known better than to start a snowball fight with a professional baseball player.

But he was laughing when she looked into his face. It was as if the cloud of sadness that was around him had finally completely lifted. All it had taken was eight inches of snow.

"Virginia?" She heard her mother's voice and scrambled off Carlos.

Her mother stood in the doorway, looking sophisticatedly relaxed in a cashmere twinset and her grandmother's diamond studs. Her father was just behind her, looking dashing with his silver hair. They were such a stark contrast to her, and she immediately felt as though she should have worn more somber colors and tied back her hair.

"Hi!" she said, her voice unnaturally high. She looked back at Carlos, who had gotten up as gracefully as a professional athlete should. "We finally made it!" She walked over to her parents and gave them each a hug.

"We?" her mother said in that voice she always used when Virginia did something unbecoming.

"Is that shortstop for the Miami Hammerheads, Carlos Bradley?" her father asked.

"Yes." She glanced back at Carlos who hovered behind her. "Mommy told you I was working for him, right?"

"Yes, sweetheart, but we almost didn't believe it."

She had opened her mouth to retort, but Carlos extended his hand to her father. "It's a pleasure to meet you, sir. Thank you for having me in your home."

"The pleasure is mine, son." Her father's face bloomed into a smile. "You are one of the most phenomenal players in the game."

"I've been out an entire season. I'm not sure about that."

"You'll go back and be phenomenal again. Please come in." Carlos followed her father inside, but Virginia's mother stayed where she was.

"We?" she asked again.

"I told you yesterday that I was going to bring my friend," Virginia said, trying to skirt the subject as she attempted to glide past her mother and into the house.

But her mother wasn't allowing that. She gripped Virginia's arms and gave her the look that she gave to unruly college freshmen after spring fling. "When you said a friend, I was imagining a girl around your age with similar interests. Not the man you're working for."

"I don't just work for him, Mother," she hissed so that the men wouldn't hear her. "He's my friend and his family is scattered all over the place for the holidays. I thought it would be nice for him to spend time with the sweet, loving family we are going to pretend to be for the next few days."

"You're not just working for him anymore?" her mother asked, one of her eyebrows raised. "And we don't have to pretend. We are a loving family, but don't act as though you were up front with all the details."

"I know. I'm sorry, but I found him. Can we keep him, please?"

"Only if you agree to take care of him."

"Thank you, Mommy." She hugged her mother again.

"I missed you, Virginia," her mother said softly. "I'm glad you're here." She picked up a lock of Virginia's hair. "I see you're still a fan of this style."

"We're letting all the cold air into the house," she said, ignoring her mother's jab.

"Yes." They went in, closing the door behind them to find the men in deep conversation. "I can see why you like this one, Virginia. Your *friend* is very handsome."

"Is he?" she asked with a straight face. "I hadn't really noticed."

Her mother gave her a pointed look, but didn't say anything. Virginia took the opportunity to walk over to Carlos and her father. "Daddy, the driveway isn't cleared. You always clear it right away. Is your back bothering you again?"

"A bit." The colonel looked at his wife. "Your mother doesn't want me to irritate it any more, even though I can push the snowblower. It's only the shoveling that would bother it. Your brother is going to do it when he comes over. He got stuck at work yesterday due to the snow."

"I can clear the driveway," Carlos volunteered.

"You can't!" her mother said in horror. "You're a guest and you just got here."

"But your son was working all night and all I did was sit on a plane, Dr. Andersen."

"But airport travel during the holidays can be very exhausting."

"We flew private," he said, as if it was normal. "Just point me in the direction of the snowblower. I'll get it cleared in no time."

"I'll help you, Carlos." Virginia stepped forward. "Mom, can you make some coffee, or better yet that really great hot chocolate you always keep around?"

"Relax, Gin." Carlos squeezed her shoulder. "Spend time with your family."

"I'll come with you, son," her father said as he grabbed his coat and gloves. "Could use the fresh air."

A moment later they were gone.

"I think your father has found a new playmate."

Virginia shrugged. "Any man would jump at the chance to hang out with him. People swarm him whenever we leave the house. He's sweet to all of them."

"Sweet?" Her mother gave her that look again. "I did some more reading up on him. He seems to have been sweet to a lot of women. None of them known for their brains and one of them seems to have been involved in some kind of sex-tape scandal."

"That has nothing to do with me, Mother," Virginia said, trying to keep her frustration at bay. "He's my friend. He's a nice guy and right now he's out there clearing your driveway. I don't care what you've heard about him. All I care about is what *I* know about him."

The front door opened again and Asa came rushing in. Thank God he was here. She wasn't sure she could remain calm through her mother's interrogation. But she was sure that it wasn't over yet. Her mother would want to know everything that Virginia didn't want to tell.

"Gin's here!" Asa grabbed her up in giant bear hug and spun her around. "You're looking beautiful, sis."

"Living on an island in the Keys and being gainfully employed agrees with me." She looked him over when he put her down. Asa was a beautiful man, superfit with a bright white smile and smooth skin the color of chocolate. "Look at you, babe. You're swollen like a tick."

"I've been working out with some of the fire fighters. They're into some intense stuff."

"You look good, Asa." She hugged him again, resting her head on his chest. "I missed you."

"I missed you, too. Was that Carlos Bradley outside shoveling snow with Dad?"

"Yes."

"I thought so." He lowered his voice and spoke into her ear. "We're going to have a talk about this later, away from Dr. Don't Do That."

"Okay." She grinned up at him. She felt safe in telling him what was going on in her head and in her heart. He was probably the only one.

Chapter 11

Carlos had thought he would be uncomfortable here. It was clear that Virginia's family hadn't expected her to bring him. But they were kind to him and went out of their way to make him feel at home. Dr. Andersen wasn't as warm as her son and husband. She was extremely polite, but she was distant. She kept looking between him and Virginia as if she was trying to figure out what was going on with them.

Virginia had introduced him as a friend, and that was the role he was playing. There were times during the day when he wanted to grab her hand or kiss her cheek, but he refrained and kept his distance. He acted as if he was just her friend.

And that was all he was. He was her friend who made love to her. Her friend who loved her. But that was it. They never talked about it. Never labeled things. But he was wondering if maybe they should. He was wondering if she might possibly want more from him.

"You want to go to a Nets game tomorrow?" Asa asked as he looked over the hand of cards he had just been dealt.

"Me?" Carlos asked, surprised by the offer from a man he had only known for a few hours.

"Yeah. A friend of mine gave me tickets to thank me for a favor. You want to go? They are pretty good seats. You're probably used to floor seats, but you can slum it for the night."

"Yeah, I would like that. It's been a long time since I've eaten a twelve-dollar hot dog."

"No, no." Asa shook his head. "We aren't eating regular hot dogs. We are going to have brisket dogs and maybe a cheddar brat, and they've got these pulled pork nachos that I've been dreaming about since I was there last."

"You going to eat all that, Asa?" Virginia walked into the dining room with pie and coffee for Asa, the colonel and him. "You're all about clean eating."

"Yes, but when I go out, I go all out. We're going to have a good time."

"It's okay with you if I go, Virginia?"

"Of course. Why wouldn't it be?"

"I don't know. We came down here so you could see your family. And now we're headed to a game without you. I want this to be okay with you."

She came over and kissed his cheek twice. "I'm not one of those women who pretends things are fine when they aren't. But you know that already, don't you?"

He wanted to pull her into his lap and kiss her, really kiss her. He hadn't made love to her since before they left and he wouldn't get to for the next few days. He missed her terribly.

"Are we going play cards, men, or are we going to blab all day?" Colonel Andersen barked.

"We're waiting for Virginia to sit her behind down so we can start."

"I went to get you pie! Don't rush me."

"I thank you for the pie. Now sit down so I can beat you."

He liked Asa. He liked the colonel. He saw his younger siblings a lot but they just felt like part of a family and not a whole one. The Andersens were a whole family, and it was nice that he got to be a small part of it, even if it was just for a just a little while.

"Can I come in?" Carlos poked his head into Virginia's childhood bedroom two evenings later. She was lying in bed on top of the covers, feeling pleasantly tired after spending a drama-free day shopping with her mother.

"Yeah. Come in." She felt that little rush she always got when she saw him. Her breath quickened; her heart lifted. She couldn't recall the last time anybody had made her feel like this. Maybe in high school with her first crush. Only with Carlos it was more intense.

"You're not going to get up?" he asked as he walked over to her.

"No, you're going to lie down." She held out her hand to him and he took it, kissing it before he settled his heavy body half on top of hers on the small twin bed.

"This bed is so small."

"You complaining?" She rubbed herself against him, relishing his closeness.

"No, I like it." He wrapped his arms around her, pulling her so close that not even air could pass between them. He just looked at her for a long moment, studying her face before he bent his head to take her mouth. It wasn't a hot kiss, but a slow one, a deep one, a kiss that made her forget that she was in her parents' home in New Jersey. A kiss that made her forget everything else because there was only him.

He was the only one who managed to do that to her.

"How was your day?" He stroked the hair out of her face.

"Fine." She slid her hands up the back of his shirt, caressing his strong back. "Kiss me again."

"I won't be able to stop myself."

"That's okay. My parents go to bed early. We'll lock the door and be really quiet."

"I respect your parents too much to do that in their house."

She sighed. "Goody Two-shoes."

He grinned. "Tell me how your day was."

"Good. We went shopping, then to dinner and the movies. It was a really boring film with subtitles, but my mother loved it and it kept her from criticizing my hair, fashion and life choices."

"Don't change anything because of what she says." He kissed the side of her neck. "And don't wear anything she buys you again. I like who you are." He kissed her neck again but a little steamier this time. "And the way you look and the choices you make."

"Let's sneak out," she moaned. "There's a hotel around the corner. We'll be back even before they know we're gone."

"No." He rested his chin on her hair. "At least, not tonight. We'll sneak away and do it in the daytime like normal people," he said, which caused her to laugh. "We've got one more day here and then we go home."

Home. She was starting to think of the oceanfront

mansion on Hideaway Island as her home. But it wasn't. She had a small apartment in the unfashionable section of Miami to go back to when his house was all done.

"And when we get there," he continued, "I'm not going to let you out of the bed for three days. You don't know all the things I want to do to you. I'm keeping a list."

"I can't wait." She snuggled into him. "How was dinner with my father and brother?"

"Your brother took us to this place that had the best damn pizza I've ever tasted. Miami has good food, but a man could gain fifty pounds hanging out with your brother."

"He's loves food more than I do. That's why he keeps himself in such great shape. He's only bad during the holidays."

"He's got to keep himself in shape for his job. He's a good guy, Gin. I'm glad I met him. I'm glad I'm here."

She was glad he was here, too. She would have missed him. They fell quiet for a few minutes, just enjoying being close to each other. She had taken for granted that on Hideaway Island she could see him whenever she wanted, touch him whenever she pleased. There she had him all to herself, but she knew that was going to come to an end soon because it wasn't reality. It was nice but temporary. People didn't live in a bubble like that.

He yawned just before he kissed her forehead. "I could fall asleep right here."

"Are you comfortable in the guest room? I know the mattress is a little soft for you."

"It's fine." He stroked his thumb along her cheek. "I've gotten used to sleeping with you every night. It feels weird to roll over and not feel you there. I think I might miss you."

He was sweet. He had his moments of pigheadedness, but this big, burly athlete was sweeter to her than anybody had ever been before, and she almost didn't know how to take it. "You *think* you miss me? I would have much preferred to hear that you're very sure you miss me and don't think you can function without me."

He cupped her face in his hands, a small smile curling his lips. "Yeah. What you said." And then he kissed her again. Softly. Expertly. Just enough to satisfy her need to be kissed.

She heard the sound of a throat clearing and looked up to see both her parents standing just inside her doorway.

"Shit," she said softly. "We're busted."

Carlos sat up quickly, his expression calm. "I'm sorry if I overstepped a line, Colonel and Dr. Andersen."

"She's thirty." Her father shrugged. "And you kept the door open. It was the same rules we had for her as a teenager. We just came to see if you two wanted to join us for coffee and pie."

"It was nice of you to ask, sir. But I don't think I can eat any more after that dinner we had."

"I know. I shouldn't have any, either." Her father may not have seemed as if he cared about what they were doing when her parents walked in on them, but she could see that her mother was not pleased.

"Virginia would like some pie," her mother said.

"Actually, Mom. I'm going to skip the pie tonight."

"Then, you can sit with me while I have mine."

Carlos gave her a look, as though he wanted to interfere, but like the smart man he was, he kept his mouth closed. "I'm going to head to bed. Good night, everyone."

"Good night, Carlos," her mother responded. "Virginia. Pie."

She had that tone in her voice that said that she wouldn't take any arguments. So Virginia got up and followed her mother into the kitchen. "I'm sorry you caught us kissing, but that was it."

"What were you thinking?"

"It was just a kiss. And I'm going to be thirty. I've lived with men before. Surely you can't be surprised by this."

"No. I'm not surprised by the kiss. I'm surprised that you haven't learned yet."

"Learned what?"

"You honestly don't know? You honestly don't know that it's a bad idea to mix business with pleasure? You don't think it's a bad idea to sleep with your boss?"

Virginia was silent for a moment, not sure how to respond. "I'm an interior designer and a grown woman. It's not as if I'm a secretary sleeping with an executive or a teacher sleeping with her principal. I'm decorating his house and I'm doing a damn good job. I think that entitles me to do what I want with no judgment from you."

"What does he see in you besides sex?"

That question caused a physical reaction in her stomach, as if she had been punched in the gut and all the air had been knocked out of her. "Is it so hard to believe that he just likes me? Is it so hard to believe that he thinks I'm smart? That we can talk to each other? That he's thinks I'm okay just the way I am, when you clearly do not?"

"Oh, no, you don't, young lady. I adore you. I think

you are talented, brilliant and beautiful. But you lack focus. You lack insight and you keep ending up with losers that hurt you."

"Carlos Bradley is anything but a loser. I won't allow you to say that about him, especially since he has been nothing but kind to you and good to me."

"He's not a loser. He's a good man. A nice man. But he's unobtainable for you. You always pick unobtainable men. Gay men and green-card seekers. And now you've gone and fallen for the holy grail of unobtainable men. Worth two hundred million dollars. Has dated woman after woman. Models, actresses, heiresses."

"So what? That has nothing to do with me."

"That has everything to do with you. Because I saw how you looked at him, Virginia. I thought it was a crush at first, but I can see you're in love with him. You have to learn to stop falling in love so easily."

"Why? Why do I have to? Who does it hurt?"

"You. Can't you see that it hurts you? That it takes a little piece out of you every time you do? Don't you know that every time some man breaks your heart you change your life, your career, your location? Where are you going to go when he ends it? Because he will end it. Once he heals and goes back into the spotlight and you two aren't stuck together in that house, things will change. And this would be okay if it was just a pleasant interlude for you, but you feel too much, too deep. You get too attached. He's going to break your heart and what are you going to do then?"

"Stop predicting my future. I wasn't expecting anything from him. Not marriage. Not children. I have no expectations."

"You have to think about your future. You can't always live in the now. You're nearly thirty and you're beautiful and you deserve stability and happiness. And don't get mad at me for wanting things for you. Don't get upset with me for seeing with clear eyes when yours continue to be cloudy."

"I don't want to talk about this. It's none of your business. My entire life you've been trying to stick me into a box that I just don't fit into. You never were supportive of what I wanted. You never had any faith in what I could do. You never gave me the benefit of the doubt. I may not have succeeded to the level that you wanted me to, but I haven't failed, either. And I don't plan to. If I do, I certainly won't come crawling back to you. So if you can't support me, the least you could do is keep your opinions to yourself."

She walked away from her mother, so mad she literally couldn't see straight. She then realized that it wasn't anger clouding her eyes, it was tears. Her father stepped out of the hallway and collected her into his arms.

She hadn't known it, but he was exactly what she needed in that moment. "I don't ever like to get involved in your love life, Virginia, but if you had to lose your head over a man, I'm glad it's him."

"You're just saying that because he shoveled the driveway."

"That did earn him some extra points in my book, but I've spent some time with him. He's a good man and he speaks well of you. If he treats you kindly, then I have nothing bad to say about the man."

"Thank you, Daddy." She pulled away from him. "I think I'm going to go to bed now."

"Okay, but just remember that if you ever need to come home, don't let pride stop you. I think I would like having you around. Your mother just wants to see you settled. She doesn't want to hurt you."

She nodded. Her mother may not have intended to hurt her, but Virginia sure as hell felt hurt.

They came home sooner than Carlos had planned, and he found himself surprisingly disappointed about it. But Virginia wasn't speaking to her mother after their argument. She wasn't speaking to anyone, really. It made sense for them to leave. They had spent a day in New York City, meeting Asa for a quick lunch before he started his shift. But she had been quiet then, barely responding to the conversation unless directly asked a question. It was so unlike her, and he missed her chatter, the way she put her positive spin on things.

It was more than just sadness or hurt that caused her words to stop flowing. She was introspective, thinking about something she clearly wasn't ready to share with him. And he felt bad, because it was his fault that she'd had the fight with her mother. If he had just stayed away, ignored that dangerous pull to be near her, none of this would have happened. Her rare visit with her family wouldn't have been ruined. But he couldn't stay away from her. He couldn't not touch her. He couldn't not kiss her lips, feel her closeness or smell her skin.

It was powerful. Whatever it was that was between them.

He hadn't heard the whole argument between Virginia and her mother, only parts toward the end when their voices had gotten loud.

He was going to move on, her mother had warned her. Once life got back to the way it was long before her, he was going to move on to somebody new.

His first thought was *no*. He couldn't just forget her. He couldn't throw her away like that. She meant too much to him.

But he remembered the missed calls on his cell phone. One from his agent. One from the team manager. He hadn't picked up, not wanting to hear what they had to say, but he already knew. His picture was in all the New York papers. He thought he had gone unnoticed at the basketball game, but he hadn't. The cameras had captured him; the headlines had said he was out of hiding.

Hiding.

He didn't like that word, but that was what he had been doing. Hiding away from his problems. Hiding away from the world. It almost made him feel cowardly. But he needed this time. He needed this time to heal. He needed this time with her, to think about other things than feeling sorry for himself, to harbor other emotions besides pain and regret.

He knew he loved Virginia. He knew there would always be a soft spot in his heart for her. But was he in love with her?

She needed stability. To put down roots. She needed to be loved by somebody who would always love her fully, who could give her everything that she wanted.

A little voice in his head whispered that he could give her that.

But he wasn't sure.

He wasn't sure if he was ready for marriage and kids. He wasn't sure if he was in the right state of mind to be her rock. He wanted to be her rock, but right now he felt as if he needed her more than she needed him. And he wanted to be there for her. He wanted to be able to give her as much as he took.

"I never thought I would miss humidity so much," she said once they got into the house. She dropped her suitcase on the floor in the kitchen and went right for the freezer. "See? You'll be glad I decided to stay up all night and remix all the Thanksgiving food. Now we'll have turkey shepherd's pie. Turkey pasta bake. I can make you a turkey, brie and cranberry sandwich. It's really good, especially when you toast the bread and put about four or five pieces of bacon on it." She pulled out a frying pan. "You must be hungry."

There she went, taking care of him again, when it should be the other way around. He wished he knew how to be there for her.

He grabbed her hand. "I can make the sandwiches. Just talk to me."

"What do you want to talk about?"

"You. Your mother. What happened last night."

"It was nothing, Carlos." She walked away from him to retrieve the bread, but he stopped her again.

"Stop and just be still for a moment."

"There's nothing to talk about! I had a fight with my mother and I don't want to talk about it with you."

With you.

Those words stuck in his chest. As though she was saying she could talk about it to anyone else but him.

He had told her everything about himself, more than he had revealed to anyone else, but she didn't want to talk to him. "I just want to know what's wrong."

"It's nothing."

"It's not nothing, damn it! It's something. It's something big because you haven't been out of your head all day."

"I can't be quiet? I can't have some time to think? You get time to think. You spent months here alone thinking. Running away from people. From the whole damn world. And I can't have a couple of hours to feel what I'm feeling? You don't get to dictate what I feel or for how long I feel it."

"I'm not! I just want to know what's up with you. I think I have earned that right."

"You really want to know? My mother thinks that you're just another bad mistake I'm making. And maybe you are. Maybe I should have never gone down this road with you but— "

"But you did and now you regret it."

"No." She shook her head. "Don't put words in my mouth. I wasn't going to say that."

"You didn't have to. It takes one conversation with your mother to shake your faith in what we have."

"What do we have anyway?" She looked him in the eye. "Tell me right now what we have, because sometimes I don't think it's very much."

"If you could look me in the eye and say that, I guess we never had anything at all." He turned to walk away.

"Carlos, don't walk away. I don't want to fight with you."

"We weren't fighting. All I wanted to do was talk to you, but you didn't. Good night."

Chapter 12

Carlos stared out of his bedroom's glass doors that overlooked the ocean. It was morning, but the sky was still dark and a full moon shone, lighting up the entire beach. The view was one of the best things about his bedroom, but it had been a while since he had seen this scene. Except for the past few days, he had spent the past few weeks waking up in Virginia's bed.

He had missed this view, but he missed Virginia more. He hadn't been able to sleep well since they went to her parents' house. He'd been looking forward to coming home last night, just so he could sleep beside her, hear her soft, slow breathing in the night, feel her smooth, warm skin against his. He still wasn't sure why he'd got so mad at her.

She had been right. What were they? What did he want from her? He'd gone into it thinking that they would just be friends who had sex. He had been involved in a situation like this before, but it hadn't affected him like this. And if he were honest with himself, he and Virginia had been more than just friends when they'd started sleeping together. He had never wanted anybody the way he wanted her. He didn't think it was possible to ever want anybody that way again, and that scared the shit out of him.

His bedroom door slowly opened and Virginia slipped inside, the dim light from the moon illuminating her. He didn't say anything as she crept toward his bed, but he felt his heart pound harder. He should have gone to her last night instead of her coming to him.

"I'm not apologizing," she said as she pulled the blankets aside and climbed on top of him. "I have nothing to be sorry for, but I don't want to fight with you. I hate fighting with you." She slid her hands over his cheeks and leaned down to kiss him, her beautiful breasts pressing against him. It was a hell of a kiss. A slow, deep, makeup kiss, even though she'd said she wasn't sorry. She shouldn't be sorry, but he was willing to fight with her more if all her makeup kisses were like this.

He slid his hands up the back of her nightgown just to feel her smooth, thick thighs. But he found that she wasn't wearing underwear as she sat straddled on top of him. He grew hard thinking about how just his boxers separated them.

She noticed his excitement. The look in her eye changed to the look she always got when she was turned on. She sat up, freed him from his shorts and slid her hand over his erection, making him even harder, if that were possible. And then she lifted herself up, biting her lip as she slid down on top of him. She was ready for him, her wetness squeezing around him, making it hard for him to keep the little bit of control he had.

"Take this off." He tugged at the hem of her nightie. "I need all of you." His voice was strained. He was so turned on he couldn't make sense of what he was saying. "I need to see all of you."

She quickly removed her nightgown, flinging it behind her. He reached up to touch her. The smooth skin of her neck, her warm chest, where her heart was beating quickly, her breasts. Her nipples were so tight with arousal that he ached to take them into his mouth.

But she wouldn't let him. She pinned his arms behind his head, placed her hands on his chest and rose up slowly, almost to the point that he was out of her. She looked him in the eye, her lip between her teeth as she did, and sank all the way down on him. And then she did it again. He lost his breath.

She was teasing him. Almost punishing him with this slow ride. He longed to grab her hips, roll her over and pump into her until he collapsed, but he knew she wouldn't allow that. That he owed it to her to let her make love to him her way.

She increased her pace, riding him faster, harder, her eyes drifting shut as she took her pleasure. A cry escaped her mouth, her orgasm coming on fast, seeming to take her by surprise. She slumped over, her breath coming in short spurts. She kissed his chest, her body liquid and boneless, all the while he was hard as steel inside her.

"Okay, baby. It's your turn."

He rolled her onto her back, wrapped her legs around his waist and lost control. He plunged into her, loving the way it sounded as their skin slapped together. His pace became frenzied and her cries grew louder. He thought it was impossible to be more turned on than he was, but hearing her cry out his name and feeling her tightness around him and her fingers dig into his back made his arousal spike to another level.

He had had good sex before, but he only had sex like this with her. And he knew that was because he loved her. He loved her so much he didn't know what to do with himself.

His climax came then and he buried himself in her one last time before he collapsed on top of her. But even then he couldn't stop himself. He kissed up the center of her throat, the side of her neck, the skin behind her ear.

"I've missed you," he whispered into her ear before he took her mouth in a long, deep kiss.

"You're not mad anymore?"

"No."

"Good. After that kind of sex, you shouldn't be."

He laughed. She made him laugh. She was the only one who could. He disconnected himself from her but pulled her into his arms to keep her close.

"During our argument, my mother said that my last boyfriend was gay. I had no idea that she thought that. I never told her we almost never had sex. I don't know why I couldn't see that."

"What did his breakup note say?"

"'I can't be who I really am with you.'" She sighed. "Oh, hell. It was obvious, wasn't it? I just don't know why somebody would spend a year of their lives with someone they didn't love."

"He loved you. There's no doubt about that." She was lovable. She was the definition of the word. "He just couldn't be with you."

"I was stupid. I'm still so stupid. My mother says I

only fall in love with unattainable men. She thinks that you're just another one of them."

"You're not stupid. Stop thinking that about yourself. I respect your mother but she doesn't know everything. You shouldn't let her shake your confidence in yourself." It then dawned on him what she'd said.

Fall in love.

You're just another one of them.

"Are you in love with me, Virginia?"

She was quiet for a long moment, and that was all the answer he needed. "I think this should be our last time, Carlos," she said softly.

He wasn't expecting those words from her and just as he was about to say something she spoke again. "I got an email that the pieces I was waiting for are on their way. I'll be done in another week or so. I've loved working here, and I'll be sad to go. I'll always have a soft spot in my heart for you and this island."

It felt as if she was breaking up with him. It almost felt as though he was suffocating. He didn't know what to say. What to tell her. There were so many thoughts in his mind, but the only one that was clear was that he didn't want her to go.

"No," he said.

"No?" She blinked up at him in confusion.

"No. This isn't our last time. This isn't the end."

"But you're the one who said when one of us wants to end it, we would."

"Why do you want to leave?"

"Because I'll be done, and no matter how wonderful this was, I have to move on with my life. That was my plan. Do this job, grow my business and move on. That was always my plan."

She had a plan. A direction for her future. He didn't have one, but he knew he wasn't ready to let her go yet.

"Fine, but today isn't our last time. We end when you're gone for good."

Now he just had to figure out how he could get her to stay.

Virginia couldn't shake the nervous feeling that gripped her as she walked around the great room removing the white drop cloths that covered the furniture Carlos had told her he didn't want to see. It hadn't been hard to hide what she had been doing from him because he didn't care what she had been doing, but after months of working there, it was finally time to see what he thought.

The house looked beautiful, exactly the vision she'd had in her mind. Sleek, masculine, worthy of any athlete in the prime of his life. It was her best work yet. A design she would be proud to place in her portfolio. She wasn't really nervous about what he would think. She was nervous because this was the end. After she showed him everything it would be time to say goodbye, time to go back to her life in her tiny apartment in her crowded neighborhood.

She would miss it there. The island. The people she had come to know. But most of all she would miss him. She had tried to end things two weeks ago, but he hadn't let her. Every night he'd taken her to bed. Every morning she'd woken up in his arms. It was going to be hard to go back to life without him. But she had to.

She had fallen in love with him when she wasn't supposed to. And while it was lovely to dream about a life together, children, a family of their own making, she knew that wasn't reality. She knew she didn't really fit into his life. And he didn't fit into hers.

She had seen the buzz starting to form. The photos of Asa and him were all over the internet. There was tons of speculation about what he was doing and when he would return. Some reports even said that he had been seen with a mysterious woman that she knew must be her. It was easy to forget that he was a hero, one of America's favorite men, when they were alone. But how long could she expect him to stay in this protective bubble?

He would go back. He would have to go back, because baseball meant the world to him. Baseball linked him to his father. She wasn't a doctor, but she could tell that he was better. He had taken to doing sprints on the beach. He ran every day. He swam. He worked out just as hard as any active player would. Maybe harder. He hadn't said that he was preparing to go back but she knew he was. He hadn't said much to her at all this past week; he'd just made love to her every night as if he was never going to see her again.

And that made this moment even more difficult. She made her way up to his bedroom to find that he had just come out of the shower. He had a towel wrapped around his waist as he rubbed lotion onto his skin.

"Come get my back," he said in way of greeting as he held out the bottle to her. She went over to him, even though she knew she shouldn't touch him now because it would make leaving him later just that much tougher. His back was hard, and slightly damp, but it felt good.

She rested her cheek against his back when she was finished. She was dangerously close to tears even though it wasn't even time to say goodbye yet.

"I'm done," she said, but the words were a struggle.

"Thank you for getting my back."

"I meant, I'm done with the house. I'm ready to show you."

"I know." He turned. Grasping the back of her neck he brought his lips down on top of hers and kissed the breath out of her. "You can show it to me in a few minutes." He yanked his towel off and tumbled her into bed.

It was nearly two hours before they emerged from his bedroom. He had made love to her twice and was now holding her hand as she showed him the rooms she had done. He remained silent. Not a word, just listened as she spoke. There wasn't a sound from him, not a head nod, not a hint of what he was thinking.

She led him down the hallway and back into the great room. He let go of her hand and walked around the room, his eyes turning critical.

"I don't like it."

"What?" His words shook her.

"The bedrooms are fine. I don't like this room or the living room. I don't like the paint in here."

"Are you kidding me? The paint is the only thing you have seen in here. You even saw them paint it and didn't have one comment."

"I don't know. I thought it would all come together when all the furniture arrived, but I don't like it. It looks too rich in here. I feel as though I'm in somebody else's house instead of my home. I want you to redo it. And do my bedroom, too."

"What are you trying to pull, Carlos?"

"Nothing." He looked around the room again. "It doesn't feel right."

"But I asked you! I asked and asked! You never had

any input. You said you didn't care as long as it looked nice. It looks nice. It looks beautiful!"

"It does. For somebody else. For my sister, maybe. Ava would love this, but I don't. I hired you to do something I would like and I want you to do it over."

"How? What do you want in here? What color paint? What kind of furniture? Do you even know? It's going to take weeks to do this over!"

"Why are you so upset, Virginia?"

"Because I poured myself into this job, into you, and you don't like it."

"It's not me."

"What do you mean by that? I had you in mind the whole time. This place is perfect for a superstar athlete, perfect for somebody like you."

"Not somebody like me. I want it for me, and I'm not a superstar, or an athlete. I'm a man who wants to live in a place that feels like home. Please do it over. Do it like you would do your own place.

"My own place? I don't understand."

"Just make it feel like home. Make it feel like a place you would want to spend the rest of your life."

She opened her mouth to ask for more clarification, but he walked away and she was left wondering what the hell she was going to do next.

That night Carlos went down the hallway that led to Virginia's room. The house was finished. It looked great, amazing, even. Virginia was a talented designer and he had no regrets about hiring her. How could he? Even if the house had looked like garbage, he couldn't regret hiring her. She had given him much more than money could buy. She had brought him some happiness when he was least expecting it. But there was something off about the house.

Having her redo it wasn't a ploy to get her to stay, even if it was true that he didn't want her to go, but the house didn't feel like a home. It felt like a showpiece. That was not what he'd wanted. Maybe he should have been more clear about he desired, but he was one of those men who didn't know what he wanted until it was right in front of his face.

He arrived at Virginia's room to find that the door was closed. This was the first time he'd found it this way since he had started spending his nights there. He turned the knob, planning to enter anyway, but it didn't move.

She had locked him out.

"Virginia?" He knocked on the door, knowing that she had been upset with him earlier, but he never thought she would lock him out. "Come on, baby. Don't lock me out."

She opened the door, but just enough so he could see her face. It appeared he was going to have to make himself comfortable in the hallway.

"If you think you're going to tell me you hate my work and then come down here and have sex with me, you've got another thing coming, Mr. Bradley. I'm not a booty call." She tried to close the door on him, but he wouldn't allow her.

"I know you're not a booty call. You're my best friend. You know me better than anyone. I have so much love for you. I didn't mean to make you feel bad about your work."

She stared at him for a long moment, a dozen emotions crossing her face, but the one that stood out for him the most was hurt. He had hurt her, and that was the last thing he wanted to do.

"I know, Carlos. I'm just not sure I can do this anymore. I don't think I can finish this job. I'm planning to leave tomorrow. I can recommend another designer for your bedroom and remodel."

"So you're going to walk out on me just because I don't like some furniture and paint?"

"I'm not walking out on you. I'm walking out on the job."

"Bullshit. You can't tell me that, after living with me for the past few months, this is just another job to you."

"It's not just a job! Of course it's not just a job. I love you, damn it. I worked hard for you and wanted you to be in love with what I did because I poured so much of myself into this job, into giving you something worthy of you. Then you tell me you don't like it and I'm left to think my best isn't good enough."

"It's two rooms, Virginia. Two damn rooms. I like the rest of it. I'm not doubting your work or your skills. Why do you think I asked you to do my bedroom? All I want you to do is make the rest of the house feel like this room. Like the inn. Someplace I don't..." He trailed off, realizing that she had just admitted to loving him. He loved her, too, but he felt as if saying the words right now would be empty, as though he was just saying them to appease her. He wanted to show her. He wanted her to know how much he meant them. He wanted to give her a reason to stay.

He could have lived with the house the way it was, but he was starting to think he couldn't live without her and he just didn't know how to put that into words.

"Someplace you don't what?" She blinked at him, confused.

"I just want you to make it feel like home. Make it feel like your home." He took her face in his hands and kissed her softly. "I don't want you to leave. Just think about staying. Sleep on it." He kissed her again and then backed away. "I'll see you in the morning."

Sleep on it. That was the last thing Carlos had said before he'd walked away from her last night. Sleep had been impossible for her. Maybe she had overreacted when he'd asked her to change things. If it were anybody else she would have just taken it in stride. She would have changed her plans. She would have redone whatever without question. But it wasn't any other client. It was Carlos. It was the man she had stupidly fallen in love with.

Her mother had been right. She always let her feelings get in the way. She had done it again. She had been prepared to walk away from him, to go back to her life to continue her business, and prove to her mother that she could still be successful even when she got her heart involved. But then Carlos had thrown her for a loop when he'd told her that he didn't like her work. It had made her feel as if she wasn't good enough. It had made her feel how her mother so often made her feel, that no matter how well she thought she had done, she had never done well enough. She had never made the right choices.

She didn't think she could go through that again. She was scared to death that she would do it all again and he still wouldn't like it. She was scared to death because she knew the longer she stayed, the harder it would be to leave. Because she was deeply in love with him and all he had said was that he had love for her.

Love for her.

Not that he was in love with her.

She had been through a lot with men, but she couldn't take it again if someone she loved didn't love her back. All the way. As much as she loved them.

Her cell phone rang just as she was about to leave her room. Her mind was still not made about what she was going to do. She had never quit a job. She had never run away. She didn't want to start now. She didn't want to be weak, but she didn't want her heart crushed, either.

"Hey, girl," Willa said when she picked up. "I got your text. Mr. Hot Baseball Player driving you crazy?"

"Yeah. I've been here for months. I asked him what he wanted. I went to him with paint options and furniture catalogs. He was with me when I picked out fixtures and he never said a word about anything. He had no opinion. And now he hates it."

"The whole house? He can't."

"No. Not the whole house. Just the common rooms. He said it doesn't feel like home. But what the hell does home feel like for him? For me? For anyone?"

"Damn, Gin. I've never heard you get so worked up over a man or a job."

"I don't know if I can do what he wants. I'm famous for getting my feelings involved. I got them too involved this time. I fell in love."

"I don't think you always get your feelings involved. You love easily, but you don't fall in love. You lived with that French guy for over a year, and instead of crying over him like most people, you changed your life."

"I followed him across the country. I left my job. I must have loved him."

"Were you *in* love with him?"

"No."

"See!"

"What's your point, Willa?"

"My point is that's it's okay if you got your feelings all tangled up. It's okay if you fell in love with a fine-ass superrich baseball player, because, girl, who wouldn't? And don't worry about what your mother thinks. She's just doing her job. She's cautious so you don't have to be."

"What am I going to do about Carlos?"

"You are going to finish this job to his satisfaction, and if he can't see how wonderful you are and if he doesn't get down on his knees and beg you to stay, then screw him. You'll have a great story to tell in the memoir I'm going to help you write. But just make sure you get one of those infamous parting gift baskets on your way out."

Virginia laughed. It was the first time in days she'd felt like doing so. "I love you, Willa."

"You should, honey. I think I'm going to be in New York for Christmas. I want to see you. It's been forever."

"I'll make sure of it. Even if you don't come home, I'll come to where you are. You are my family, too."

A few minutes later they disconnected and Virginia felt steady enough to leave the safety of her room and face him. Willa had put everything into perspective for her. If all she got out of this experience was a good paycheck and a couple of months of sex with a man she loved, she had gotten more than she had ever dreamed of.

She had let the argument with her mother shake her confidence. But she was a good interior designer. She just had to learn to give him what he wanted.

She opened her door, losing her breath as she saw what was in the hallway. Canvases. Large, high-quality, blank canvases that had been impossible to find on the island. There were smaller ones, too, and paint. Beautiful, richly colored oil paint. The kind she used when she was at her best. Every supply she could ever need was sitting there in front of her. Smocks, easels, brushes. Her heart pounded faster.

He had done this. He had done this for her, but how? Why?

She ran up the hallway to find him. He was in the great room, looking up at the picture she had chosen for the spot above the fireplace.

"I couldn't put my finger on what was wrong with this room," he said. He must have heard her come in. "There's no you in here. You put somebody else's art in here. You put this stupid picture of... What the hell is this?"

"It's an abstract. It's called *Fjord in the Morning*. I picked it because it went with the color scheme."

"It's stupid, is what it is." He glanced back at her. "I looked you up. When you told me you used to be a painter I had no idea that you've sold your pieces all over the world. You're known for your use of color and your realistic style. An article said in a world of wannabes and posers you're the real thing. Now, how could I have the real thing in my house and not have her give me the one thing I can't find anywhere else?"

"How did you do it?" she asked, breathless. Her heart was beating so hard she could barely hear her own thoughts. "How did you get all of that stuff here?"

"I'm blessed."

"You're rich," she countered, and she couldn't help but smile.

"I just want you to paint, Virginia. I saw your work at the inn. I don't know a damn thing about art, but I know you have a gift. I know that when I come to this house I want to be welcomed by your work."

She didn't know what to say. Instead, she walked her behind him and buried her face in his back.

"There's a photographer coming from *Miami Home.* She's going to do a spread on this house."

"What?" She walked around to face him. "Why?"

"Your work deserves to be showcased. And think of how good it will feel to tell your mother that you've got twenty jobs lined up, all because you slept with me."

"She'll accuse me of sleeping my way to the top."

He shrugged. "It's better than sleeping your way to the bottom."

A laugh escaped her throat. "I love you, Carlos." Those words escaped too easily. She hadn't meant to say them. But she didn't want to take them back, either. Carlos should know that he was loved.

He grabbed her hips and pulled her into him. "I want you to stay here with me. I want to be with you." He slid his hands into her hair, brought her lips to his and kissed her deeply. "I guess I'm saying that I don't want to be your friend anymore."

"Oh? I think I stopped being your friend a long time ago."

"Really?" He grinned at her. "I never wanted to be your friend in the first place."

"Take me to bed, then. I need to see how people who aren't friends make love."

Chapter 13

A month had passed. Christmas had come and gone. It was the first time they had been apart since Virginia had come to Hideaway Island. She had gone to spend the holiday with her best friend Willa, and he had taken his siblings to spend a few days with his mother, who was stateside after spending most of the winter in Costa Rica.

He had gotten to visit with his older sister and her family. He had spent time with his mother, who still had sadness in her eyes when she looked at him because he reminded her of his father.

But, despite that, he had had a nice time. Though part of him had felt a little empty. He had missed Virginia. He hadn't been sure if he would. He'd thought he might welcome the space from her since they spent every day together. It had been like that with every other woman. He would look forward to time on the road so he could have time to himself, but it was the opposite with her. He had even cut his trip short so that he could go home to her.

They had been together in the house, but she had spent her mornings painting in private and her afternoons redoing the rooms he had asked her to. She was completely overhauling them. The walls had gone from that cream color to a soft ocean blue. She had gotten rid of the sleek furniture, the things that screamed to the world that a flashy millionaire lived there.

She had even started taking small jobs on the island. More recently, she was working with the senior citizens' community center, redoing their dining room. She had carved out her own life here on the island and she was happy. Her happiness was contagious, because he hadn't felt *this* good in years. So healthy. It was why he was afraid to tell her what he was going to tell her.

He walked into the billiards room, which she had turned into a makeshift studio since Carlos had never enjoyed pool. She was painting, and for a moment he silently watched her work. He'd never thought watching somebody paint could be entertaining, but it was with her. Especially when she worked with such a large canvas. It was as if she was using her entire body with each brushstroke.

She was working on the sky at sunset. There must have been a hundred colors in the sunset alone, and below it was the beach that was right outside their home with a single man overlooking the ocean. The way she had the light hitting the man made it seem as if there was magic around him.

"That's beautiful, Gin."

She turned around and smiled at him. There was paint smudged on her cheeks. "I'm very fond of this one." She picked up a photograph and handed it to him. It was of his father in his younger days. He was standing on the beach, facing the camera, a big grin on his face. "I think he would like to look over the ocean."

He didn't know what to say so he hugged her tightly, now wondering if he should even bother to tell her his news at all. "How did you get that picture?"

"Your mother sent it. She sent me a bunch. Didn't she tell you?"

"No. You spoke to her?"

"She called while you were at the doctor. I like her, Carlos."

"I'm sure she likes you, too." He paused for a moment. "I came here to tell you something about my doctor's appointment."

She looked up at him, her face full of concern. "Are you okay?"

"Yes, that's just it. I'm in the best shape of my life, he said. My Achilles is fully healed. He thinks I can go back for spring training."

"That's great!" She threw her arms around him and held onto him. "That's great, right?"

"He's just the local doctor. I have to see the team's specialist in Miami before I'll know for sure. My agent wants me to come back for some meetings that I've been putting off."

"Meetings about what?"

"My career. Even if I do go back, Virginia, I need to start thinking about life after baseball. I have to do something. I've been on vacation for a year."

"I wouldn't call this last year a vacation. You took two classes. You got As in the both of them. You worked so hard."

"I know, but I need to do more."

"I understand," she said after a moment, but he wasn't so sure she did. "When are you leaving for Miami?"

"I want you to come with me." He'd lied. It was more than a want. It was a need. He needed her there with him. He hadn't been back since his surgery. He hadn't seen any of his old friends, his teammates, the swarms of fans he used to encounter every day. It was like going back in time, like going back to another life, and he wanted her there beside him so he didn't forget this life that he had. The life he had really come to love as much as playing baseball.

"Of course I'll go with you. When do we leave?"

"Hey, Carlos! You coming back? We miss you, dude!" a man screamed at them from across the street. Virginia mentally shook her head. It wasn't *them* he was screaming at, it was Carlos. Everywhere they had gone somebody was yelling at them, coming up to them.

And it started the moment they'd stepped off the plane. Most of the people who came up to him were adoring and in awe that they were in the presence of their hero. Some of them peppered him with questions and pushed things in his face to sign. She had to give it to Carlos, he had been kind and gracious to everyone, thanking them for their support, treating each of them as though they were important.

He wasn't the man she was used to being with; it was as if he had on some kind of armor. His smile served as his uniform when they were out in public. He must be exhausted. She didn't know if she could be him. She didn't know if she could keep up her good nature all day long. She hadn't understood why the world loved him so much. She knew he was a baseball player and a good one. But he was a good man. And in Miami he was like everyone's brother, son or friend.

She slipped her hand into his, locked their fingers. He looked down at her, pausing a moment to kiss her forehead. "I'm sorry, baby."

"For what?"

"For this. It's taken us an hour to get down the street."

"It has, but I guess this is all part of being you, isn't it?"

"It's not always this bad. It's just because I've been gone for so long. It's usually only like this when the Hammerheads are heading into the playoffs or the World Series."

"There's all this buzz around you. I'm afraid Miami is going explode with happiness when they find out you're going back. There might even be a parade."

He smiled softly. "I doubt it. And we don't know if I'm going back yet."

"I know you're going back. Why don't you?"

"Because I have wanted to go back for so long that if something happens and I can't, I don't want to be knocked on my ass by it, like I was last time."

"You don't want to be disappointed. I understand that."

"Let's not talk about it," he said as they walked up to the restaurant they were heading to. "Let's talk about the seafood paella we are about to have."

"Mr. Bradley!" The hostess's face lit up when she saw him. "Welcome back. We're so glad to see you again." She looked up at him with a flirtatious smile on her face. "A few of our girls have quit since you stopped coming around. They said the view had gotten dull."

Carlos laughed good-naturedly. "Sorry to hear that. You know I couldn't be in town without coming to my favorite place. I've been telling my girlfriend all about the food here."

When the hostess's eye went to Virginia, it was as if the woman was seeing her for the first time. That was something Virginia was going to have to get used to. Since she had been back in Miami with Carlos it was as though she was invisible. She had lived here for over a year, worked in the homes here, spent time in this neighborhood, and yet she felt like a stranger in her own town.

"Well." The hostess's smile turned more professional and a little less flirty. "Welcome to Costado's. We hope you have a good time tonight."

"Thank you," Virginia said as the woman turned to show them to their table. The restaurant was nice but by no means fancy. The decor was simple, the lighting dim and the view from the window was of a regular neighborhood street instead of the flashy downtown area she had expected when he'd told her he wanted to go out for dinner.

It made her feel kind of silly that she'd gone into her design for his house with single-minded focus. She had decided on the design before she'd got to know him. He was a humble man, a no-flash, no-frills kind of guy. It was probably why everyone loved him so much.

The waiter came, taking their order and chatting them up about the Hammerheads' past season. She hadn't seen Carlos watch one game, but he was up on his team's record.

When the waiter left, they were alone again. They hadn't been alone all day. He had been in business meetings for hours. And there had been fans coming up to him. They had barely spoken since that morning. She had taken for granted that she could see him anytime she wanted to when they were back on the island. Now she was in competition for his attention. She was beginning to feel as though that was a competition she couldn't win.

She didn't blame him. It wasn't his fault; this was his life. She couldn't say she hadn't expected it. She'd known. She had always known. She'd just pushed it into the back of her mind, because she'd never thought she would be here with him.

"How was your day?" she asked, curious about what he had done all day.

"Let's talk about your day first. How does it feel to be back?"

"I was going to ask you the same thing."

"Yo, Carlos!" A man walked up to them, grinning from ear to ear. Carlos grinned back. Not one of those smiles he gave fans, but a genuine happy smile. She figured he must know the man. "I heard you were back." He slapped him hard on the back. "The locker room's not the same without you, boy. When are you bringing your old ass back? We've missed you."

"Just waiting on the doctor to clear me."

"When do you go?"

"In a couple of days."

"They've got to clear you." He looked over to Virginia. "I'm sorry, honey. I didn't mean to interrupt. We're old friends."

"This is my girlfriend, Virginia. Virginia, this is Vito Martinez, best damn pitcher we've ever had."

"It's nice to meet you, Vito." She reached out her hand to shake his.

"So this is your girl." Vito grinned at her and then looked back to Carlos. "My girl was telling me that she read you were seen with somebody, but I thought it was because you're always seen with somebody. But you've got the real thing here. You've got a woman. I'm impressed."

"Why don't you pull up a seat and join us, Vito?" she asked, knowing that the men wanted to catch up.

"You sure, Gin?" Carlos asked.

"Of course. Please join us."

"I've got Drew here with me. He's the third baseman," he said for Virginia's benefit.

"Drew's here?" Carlos looked around and she could tell he was happy to know that another friend was there. "Tell him to bring his ass over here."

A few moments later two more chairs arrived, along with another very good-looking baseball player. Virginia spent the rest of her evening listening to men talk about sports.

"Extend your foot for me," the team's doctor said to him as he studied Carlos's heel. He bent Carlos's toe back gently. "How does that feel?"

"Fine. No pain." It was so unlike the months he had spent before.

"Good." The doctor bent it back again. "Good. Stand up for me. We're going to do a soleus heel drop. Remember how to do that?"

"Yes, sir." He had done ninety of them a day since he had gotten hurt. He stood on a step and raised and lowered his leg at a forty-five degree angle, stretching his leg.

"No pain, no pull, no twinge?"

"No. I feel great."

"You look great, too. I looked at your MRI and X-rays. Your body is in better shape than before you left. You were falling apart. You worked your body too hard. I guess you needed the break."

He looked over at Virginia, who was sitting silently in the corner watching. Her face was neutral and he wondered what she was thinking. She had been so sure all along that he was going to go back, and it looked as though he was finally about to receive his confirmation.

Why the hell wasn't he happier about it?

"The team will be extremely happy to hear you're coming back."

"So it's official?"

"It's official. You're cleared. I'll notify the front office right now."

"Congratulations, baby!" Virginia stood up and hugged him tightly. He knew she was happy for him. He could never accuse her of being unsupportive, but she wasn't really happy. They had been there for a week now and he had been incredibly busy as he'd stepped back into his old life.

She was there with him, but he felt as if he hadn't seen her, as if she had taken a backseat to the rest of his life. His agent had lined up endorsement deals, appearances, commercials. He was going to be the guest of honor at a charity ball. All in preparation for his comeback.

He was told he couldn't come back quietly the way he wanted to. His fans had been waiting. His fans expected more. They had been heartbroken when he had gotten hurt. He was told he owed it to them to make his comeback special, an event.

In a way he felt beholden to them. They had supported him. They had loved him and he could tell that this city had missed him just by the warm welcome he had received when he returned. He didn't want to let them down. Baseball had been his only career. He had owed it to them and to his father to finish up on top.

But he felt as if he owed Virginia something, too. She had been coming in second all week, and that wasn't fair to her, especially when she had done so much for him.

"Thank you for being here for me."

"Of course."

"I want to take you out to celebrate."

"Oh?"

"You don't want to go out?"

"I'd rather we stay in and celebrate. I can cook for you. We can try out that big hot tub in your condo. We can spend the day in bed tomorrow."

He had an early meeting, but he chose not to tell her about it. It could be canceled. She deserved his time. His undivided attention, even if it was just for the day. Every time they left his condo they were assaulted with kindness and questions and well wishes. People interrupted their dinners, stopped them as they walked down the street. Sometimes it was annoying, but he could never be rude to them. They made his career.

Carlos Bradley's New Girl?

That was the headline of Miami's biggest paper the two mornings later. Nothing about his return. It hadn't been announced yet, but it would be later that day at a press conference, followed by a party in his honor.

She hadn't been looking forward to it, but she would have gone for him. Because it was important to him. And he was important to her. But she still couldn't muster up any excitement, because it felt as though the end was coming. The real end of them.

Last night at dinner a woman had sat down in his lap, wrapped her arms around him and kissed the side of his neck, and she had done it right in front of Virginia. She had recognized the woman, a singer from some girl group. One of those flawlessly made-up women with a perfect body. She had seen Virginia there, looked her in the eye and still sat on his lap, as if she didn't care, as if Virginia didn't matter.

Carlos had been good about it. He'd removed the woman from his lap. "That's my girlfriend across the table, and right now you are disrespecting yourself and her. Go back to where you were."

"You think you're special, honey?" the girl had asked Virginia. "You're just like the rest of us."

That experience had left her uneasy, but this morning, seeing full-color pictures of herself in the paper was another thing. It seemed that she had been followed wherever she went the past week, even when she wasn't with Carlos. Pictures of her going into the grocery store, pictures of her having lunch with Mrs. Westerfield, who was back from her trip.

That alone would have made her feel violated, but there was an article about her entire life, her career as a painter and the artist she had dated when she was much younger, a man twenty years her senior whom she had posed nude for. She didn't know how they'd found that out, she didn't know why they cared, but the article painted her as some erratic, artistic wannabe. It made it seem as though she was nowhere good enough for the town's favorite player.

"Virginia!" Carlos was standing right behind her. She hadn't heard him walk into the kitchen. "What are you reading?"

"Nothing." She tried to toss the paper aside but he grabbed it from her. She had seen Carlos angry before, but he usually went cold and silent. This time she could see it twisted in his face, feeling the hot anger roll off him.

"This is trashy garbage. They are just trying to sell papers."

"They dug into my life. They know about my first boyfriend. They printed the picture I posed for."

"Relax, baby." Carlos grabbed her hands, and it was then he noticed she was shaking. "You don't need to worry. Nobody that matters cares about this."

"I care," she said slowly as she looked up into his eyes. "I want to be here with you, but I don't think I can."

"What?" His body went still.

"I don't belong here. In your life." She shook her head. "In *this* life."

"What the hell does that mean?"

"I love you, but I'm not cut out to be a superstar's girlfriend. I'm not ready to give up everything I have worked for and melt into the background of your life."

"But you won't. I—"

"This is a big moment in your life and in your career. It's your comeback season. Everything you have wanted for the past year is about to happen, and it's going to be amazing for you, and I feel as though I'm in the way."

"You're not in the way."

"I am. I've literally been pushed out of the way so people can get to you. I'm not complaining. I'm not even suggesting that I should come first. Baseball is your first love and I want you to have it back."

"What are you saying?"

"I'm going to go home." She shook her head. "I'm going to go back to Hideaway Island. I'm going to finish your house and then I'm going to move on. Just like I was supposed to. Just like I had planned. I have given up things for men before. I have quit jobs and moved across country. I have put my happiness aside for theirs, but I'm not sure I can do that again. I love you, but I can't be in another relationship that I know is stamped with an expiration date. It wouldn't be fair to you if I did."

"But, Gin…"

"This is for the best." She stepped forward, softly kissed his lips before she backed away. "This is your time now. Enjoy it. And always remember how proud of you I am."

He was back officially. His team had held a press conference. He had been peppered with question after question from reporters. He couldn't remember any of them. It had all been a blur except for one question.

Are you happy to be back?

He had said yes, but it was a lie, because Virginia had left him. He didn't blame her. Three weeks had passed since she'd left, since the announcement had been made, since his life had changed again.

His team had to hire security for him. He had always had people come up to him when he left his house, but now there were more—there were swarms of them—and reporters and photographers. He didn't blame Virginia for wanting to escape all this, for preferring a quiet life on that little island where she had become part of the community.

He was mad at her for going. He almost felt abandoned, but he didn't blame her, because she hadn't signed on for this. She had come into his life to decorate his place. She hadn't planned on him falling in love with her.

His phone rang. It never stopped ringing these days. Even though he had an agent and a publicist, people still called him, most of them offering congratulations and well wishes. He ignored most of them, checking the caller ID only to see if it was Virginia calling. This should be the happiest time of his life—he had gotten back the thing he had wanted most this past year—but instead he was holed up in his condo waiting for her to call.

But it wasn't her. It was his mother this time.

"Hello, Mama."

"Hello, *mijo*. I haven't heard from you since the day you told me you had been cleared to play."

"I've been busy."

"Have you?" she asked in that tone of voice that told him she knew he was lying.

"There's a lot going on."

"Virginia is not with you?"

"No." He nearly choked on the word. "She left me. Some reporters dug into her past and followed her around town. I think this life is too much for her."

"She's a talented girl. She sent me pictures of the house. It beautiful. She invited me to come see it."

"You should come, Mama. I miss you."

"It's been hard for me to be there, because everything reminds me of your father. He was the last man I had ever thought I wanted, but he ended up being the only man I ever needed."

Carlos was quiet. It was hard for him to speak when there was such pain in his mother's voice.

"She sent me a painting, you know. One of your father on the beach. I cried when I saw it. Sobbed for three hours. She captured him. She never met him and yet she captured who he was with strokes of a paintbrush."

"I saw it. It's my favorite."

"I called her to thank her and ask her how she could

do that. How she could make me feel so much with one painting. Do you know what she told me? She told me that what she feels goes into her work and she thought about you the whole time she painted it. That knowing you made her work better."

"She did?"

"She loves you, Carlos. Probably more than you deserve."

She was right. He knew he had been hard to deal with, hard to live with. Virginia had given so much of herself to him already. It was selfish of him to ask her to give him any more.

"So my next question, *mijo*, is when can I expect to meet my first grandchild?"

"She left me, Ma. She doesn't want this life."

"Of course not. She wants a life that you two make together. If you let her go, you'll regret it. I've never been disappointed in you, not once, but if you let this girl go, I will be. Money is nice. Baseball is good, but love is forever, and the only thing a mother really wants for her child is to be happy. Virginia will make you happy. Please don't let this chance slip through your fingers."

Virginia packed up the last of her things and took one last look around the bedroom she had spent the past few months living in. Of all of the places she had left, this was the only one that hurt her to leave. But it was time to go. The house was finished. It was her best work. The best she could do. She'd left her mark on it. Literally. She had painted the walls herself, hung up her art in each room. She had lost herself in this project. She had lost her heart, too, but she regretted none of it.

It was time to move on. To go back. To find her next

job. To work on her next piece. She was going to paint again. She was going to show her work. She had taken this job to keep her design firm afloat, but Carlos had given her the confidence she needed to do the thing she'd loved all along.

She left the room, rolling her suitcase behind her. She had left a message for Carlos last night to tell him that she was leaving. She knew she should show him the house again, go through the changes she had made, but she couldn't bring herself to face him. It would hurt too much.

Baseball was his life. She had watched the press conference, seen how everyone had reacted to the news of his return. They were happy. He made millions of people happy just by walking onto a field. He couldn't let them down. Baseball was his destiny. And hers... She wasn't sure what hers was yet. But she was going to find it.

She heard the front door open as she walked toward it. A driver was coming to get her, to take her to the airport, but she didn't think he would just let himself into the house.

"Virginia!" Her mother walked in. "I can see why you fell in love with this island. I've been all over the world, but I don't think I have ever been to a place so beautiful."

Virginia stood there, frozen to her spot. Her mother was there.

But why? They hadn't left things on good terms, but there she was with her hair loose, wearing a long floral-print dress and a smile on her face.

"What are you doing here?"

"Carlos invited us."

"Us?" She blinked. "Carlos?"

"Flew us in private." Her father walked in with two large suitcases.

"Yes, he's a wonderful man. Flew to New Jersey himself to invite us to stay."

"Stay? But I'm leaving. I'm going home. I broke up with him because I was giving up my life to make another man happy. Isn't that what you wanted?"

"Me?" Her mother pointed to herself. "Either I was wrong or you are mistaken. I really like him, Virginia. He's very intelligent."

"He's not smarter than me." Elias walked in with a small duffel bag. Ava followed him inside with a very large designer suitcase.

"Just because you're a surgeon doesn't mean you're smarter than anybody else."

"Yeah, Ava. I think that's exactly what that means."

"Children…" A woman Virginia had never met before walked into the house. She didn't need to be introduced for Virginia to know who she was. The beautiful woman looked just like Ava.

"Mrs. Bradley." Virginia's eyes started to fill up with tears. "You're here."

"You invited me." Carlos's mother wrapped her arms around Virginia. "It's so nice to meet the woman who turned my son back into a human." She lowered her voice to a whisper. "Thank you, my sweet girl."

"I should say thank you, too." She heard Carlos's voice, and when she opened her eyes he was standing right behind his mother. "It's lucky that I started organizing this get-together before you called me last night to tell me that you were leaving. It's kind of sneaky of you. I thought you would at least give me one last goodbye."

"It wasn't sneaky. It was cowardly. I was scared that if I saw you I wouldn't be able to say goodbye."

"Well, that's a good thing for me." He got down on one knee before her. "Because I don't want you to say goodbye."

"What are you doing?" she asked as the tears slipped down her face.

"I love you. Ridiculously. Tremendously. There's not a word I can think of that can describe it. I want to spend my life here with you. I want to make a family with you. And I promise that I will devote the rest of my days to making you happy. You were there for me—it's time I give up something and be there for you."

"Give up something?" She shook her head, her heart pounding so hard it hurt. "What are you talking about?"

"Baseball." He pulled a ring out of his pocket and slipped it onto her finger. "I thought I needed it to be happy, but I can't be happy without you. Marry me, Virginia."

"No!"

"No?" she heard in unison all around her.

"You can't give up baseball. You worked so hard to get where you are. The whole state has been waiting for your return. You mean something to them, to those people, to those children who look up to you. You can't walk away from them."

"I can't let you go, either. I had to make a decision—do the right thing for the people who love me for what I can do, or do the right the thing for the woman who loves me for who I am. It wasn't a tough decision to make. In fact, it was the easiest one of my life."

"I don't want you to give it up." She got down on her knees and wrapped her arms around him, hugging him tightly to her. She'd missed him. She had felt empty without him. "I'll marry you, but I don't want you to give it up. It would be crazy of you to give it up, even though it's the sweetest, most generous thing anyone has ever done for me."

"I want you to be happy, Gin. Miami didn't make you happy. That life won't make you happy. I want you to be in a place where you love doing something you love."

"But I won't be happy if you can't do what you love. I love you too much for that. I won't allow you to. We'll just have to figure something out."

He cupped her face in his hands and looked into her eyes. "Is that a yes?"

"It's a yes."

He leaned forward and kissed her then, and it was the kiss that started the rest of their life together.

* * * * *

The one you can't resist...

Lindsay Evans

Untamed LOVE

A winning bid at an auction gets Mella Davis more than just complimentary services from landscape architect Victor Raphael. It sparks an instantaneous attraction to the brooding bachelor that takes her by surprise. Ever since love burned him in the past, nothing has cracked Victor's calm control. Opposites attract, but can they also overcome their differences...and sow the seeds of a thrilling and lasting love?

Available February 2016!

HARLEQUIN®
www.Harlequin.com

KPLE1390216

REQUEST YOUR FREE BOOKS!

2 FREE NOVELS
PLUS 2 *FREE GIFTS!*

KIMANI™
ROMANCE

Love's ultimate destination!

Turn your love of reading into rewards you'll love with
Harlequin My Rewards

"I understand whenever a Steele sees a woman he wants, he goes after her. It appears Tyson's targeted you, Hunter," Mo said as she leaned over. "Maybe he thinks there's unfinished business between the two of you."

It took less than a minute for Tyson to reach their table. He glanced around and smiled at everyone. "Evening, ladies." And then his gaze returned to hers and he said, "Hello, Hunter. It's been a while."

Hunter inhaled deeply, surprised that he had remembered her after all. But what really captured her attention were his features. He was still sinfully handsome, with skin the color of creamy chocolate and a mouth that was shaped too darn beautifully to belong to any man. And his voice was richer and a lot deeper than she'd remembered.

Before she could respond to what he'd said, Mo and Kat thanked him for the drinks as they stood. Hunter looked at them. "Where are you two going?" she asked.

"Kat and I thought we'd move closer to that big-screen television to catch the last part of the basketball game. I think my team is winning."

As soon as they grabbed their drinks off the table and walked away, Tyson didn't waste time claiming one of the vacated seats. Hunter glanced over and met his gaze while thinking that the only thing worse than being deserted was being deserted and left with a Steele.

She took a sip of her drink and then said, "I want to thank you for my drink, as well. That was nice of you."

"I'm a nice person."

The jury is still out on that, she thought. "I'm surprised you remember me, Tyson."

He chuckled, and the sound was so stimulating it seemed to graze her skin. "Trust me. I remember you. And do you know what I remember most of all?"

"No, what?"

He leaned over the table as if to make sure his next words were for her ears only. "The fact that we never slept together."

Don't miss
POSSESSED BY PASSION
by Brenda Jackson,
available March 2016 wherever
Harlequin® Kimani Romance™
books and ebooks are sold!